RAMPART
P R E S S ®

HOLIDAZE ™

CREATED BY
JUSTIN MURPHY

JUSTIN MURPHY

HOLIDAZE

FOR TREY,

MAY THE MAGIC OF THE HOLIDAYS
ALWAYS BRING YOU JOY AND LAUGHTER.

RAMPART
P R E S S

Graphically novel.

PO BOX 551056
JACKSONVILLE, FL 32255
STORY & ART BY JUSTIN MURPHY
COVER COLORING BY J. BROWN

WWW.RAMPARTPRESS.COM

ISBN: 0-9799579-1-5

FIRST PRINTING, DECEMBER 2010. PRINTED IN CANADA.

FOREWORD
(OR A RANT, IF YOU PREFER)

PEANUTS, GARFIELD, THE FAR SIDE; THEY WERE SOME OF MY FAVORITES. I REMEMBER THOSE WORKS OF ILLUSTRATED GENIUS STARING BACK AT ME FROM THE POROUS NEWSPRINT OF THE SUNDAY PAPER. HUMOR COMIC STRIPS ALWAYS HELD A NOSTALGIC PLACE FOR ME. AS A YOUNG KID, I DREAMED OF ONE DAY CREATING MY OWN STRIP AND SELLING IT FOR PUBLICATION IN NEWSPAPERS ALL OVER THE UNITED STATES. I BELIEVE MOST CARTOONISTS WOULD AGREE THAT HAVING A STRIP IN SYNDICATION IS A DREAM BEYOND ALL DREAMS. WHO WOULDN'T WANT TO BE THE NEXT CHARLES SCHULZ OR JIM DAVIS?

WELL, I'M UNDER NO ILLUSIONS. WITH AGE COMES WISDOM, AND USUALLY A STRONGER GRASP OF REALITY, AND IT TOOK ME YEARS TO REALIZE THAT SELLING A COMIC STRIP FOR NATIONAL SYNDICATION IS ABOUT AS LIKELY AS WINNING THE STATE LOTTERY. THOUSANDS OF NEW CONCEPTS ARE SUBMITTED AND THE SYNDICATES USUALLY ACCEPT ONLY A COUPLE NEW STRIPS A YEAR, AND THAT DECISION IS BASED SOLELY ON CURRENT TRENDS IN THE MARKET AND WHAT THEY THINK THE PAPERS WILL BUY. IT'S A BUSINESS, PLAIN AND SIMPLE, AND IF YOUR CONCEPT DOESN'T FIT THEIR BUSINESS PLAN, YOUR SUBMISSION GOES STRAIGHT INTO THE WASTE BASKET. IMAGINE ALL THE GREAT CARTOONS THAT WILL NEVER SEE THE LIGHT OF DAY BECAUSE THEY WERE NOT PICKED UP BY A SYNDICATE.

SO WHAT IS A FRUSTRATED CARTOONIST TO DO? WELL...WE DO WHAT WE ALWAYS DO WHEN NO ONE WILL BUY OUR IDEAS; WE SELF-PUBLISH.

HOLIDAZE IS AN EXERCISE IN FUN (OR A THERAPEUTIC RELEASE FOR A FRUSTRATED ARTIST, DEPENDING ON HOW YOU LOOK AT IT). NO, YOU WILL NOT SEE IT PRINTED IN YOUR LOCAL NEWSPAPER OR GRACING THE FRONT COVER OF YOUR NEXT BIRTHDAY CARD. THINK OF IT IS AS A MODEST ATTEMPT AT SELF-SYNDICATION. MY ONLY AVENUE, IF YOU WILL, OF STEALING A TINY SPOT IN THE LONG LIST OF CARTOON HUMORISTS. IT'S NOT JUST A TRIBUTE TO ALL THE GREAT COMIC STRIPS I READ AS A CHILD, BUT ALSO A NOD TO ALL THE HOLIDAY ICONS THAT WE CELEBRATE EACH YEAR (SEE PAGES 74 & 75 FOR CHARACTER DESCRIPTIONS). IT IS MY SINCERE HOPE THAT YOU FIND JOY IN THE WHIMSY, SARCASM AND SILLINESS WITHIN THE PAGES OF THIS BOOK.

WITH THAT BEING SAID, THANK YOU FOR GIVING IT A SHOT AND BY ALL MEANS...ENJOY!

JUSTIN MURPHY

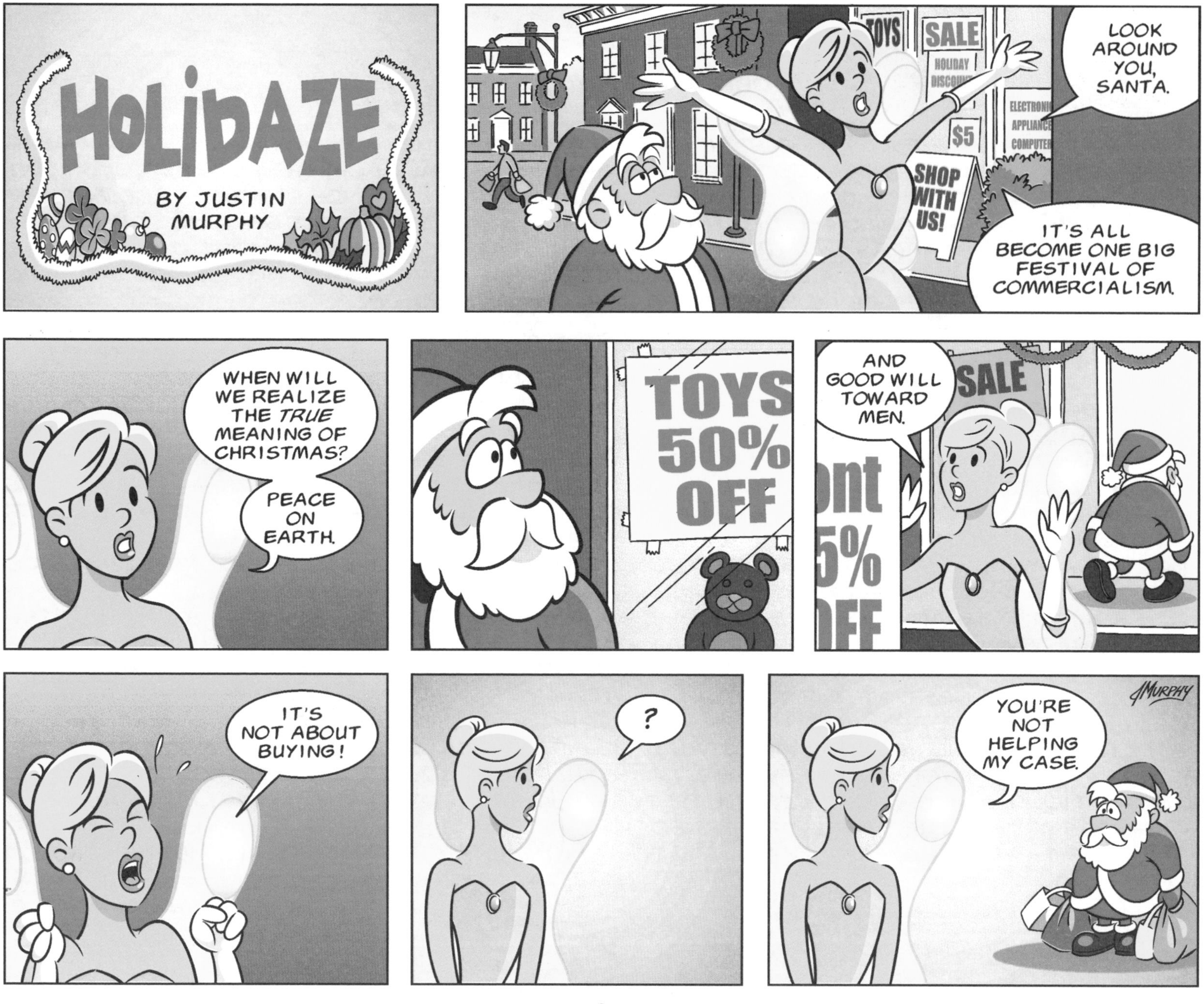
HOLIDAZE
BY JUSTIN MURPHY
TOYS
SALE
HOLIDAY DISCOU
ELECTRONI
APPLIANCE
COMPUTER
$5
SHOP WITH US!
LOOK AROUND YOU, SANTA.
IT'S ALL BECOME ONE BIG FESTIVAL OF COMMERCIALISM.
WHEN WILL WE REALIZE THE *TRUE* MEANING OF CHRISTMAS?
PEACE ON EARTH.
TOYS 50% OFF
AND GOOD WILL TOWARD MEN.
SALE
IT'S NOT ABOUT BUYING!
?
YOU'RE NOT HELPING MY CASE.
J MURPHY

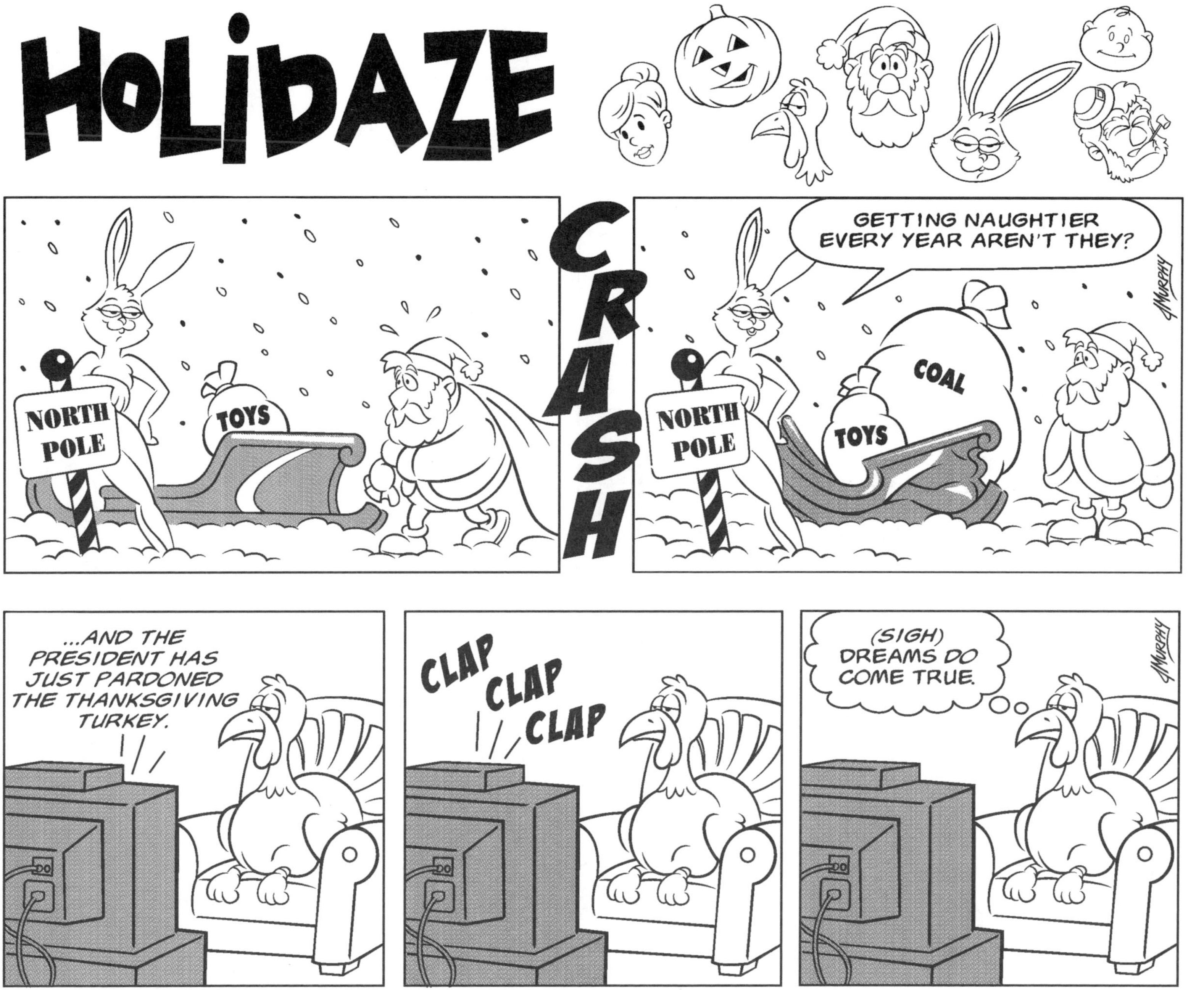
HOLIDAZE
NORTH POLE
TOYS
CRASH
GETTING NAUGHTIER EVERY YEAR AREN'T THEY?
NORTH POLE
TOYS
COAL
J MURPHY
...AND THE PRESIDENT HAS JUST PARDONED THE THANKSGIVING TURKEY.
CLAP
CLAP
CLAP
(SIGH) DREAMS DO COME TRUE.
J MURPHY

HOLIDAZE

NOW BOBBY, IT'S NOT VERY NICE TO CUT IN FRONT OF THE LINE LIKE THAT.

HAVEN'T YOU EVER HEARD OF A FAST PASS?

I LOVE EASTER. PAINTING EGGS IS MY FAVORITE PART, THOUGH I MUST ADMIT IT'S A LITTLE STRANGE.

BUNNY WHAT DO YOU FIND STRANGE ABOUT EASTER?

SEEING MYSELF EATEN IN CHOCOLATE EFFIGY.

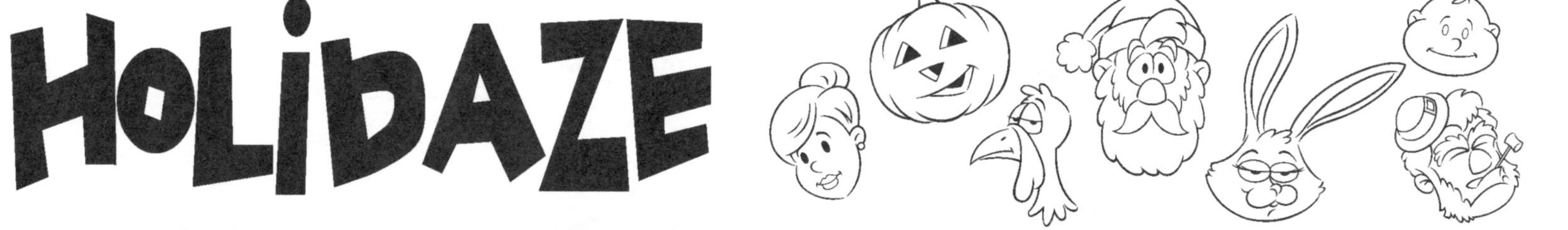
HOLIDAZE

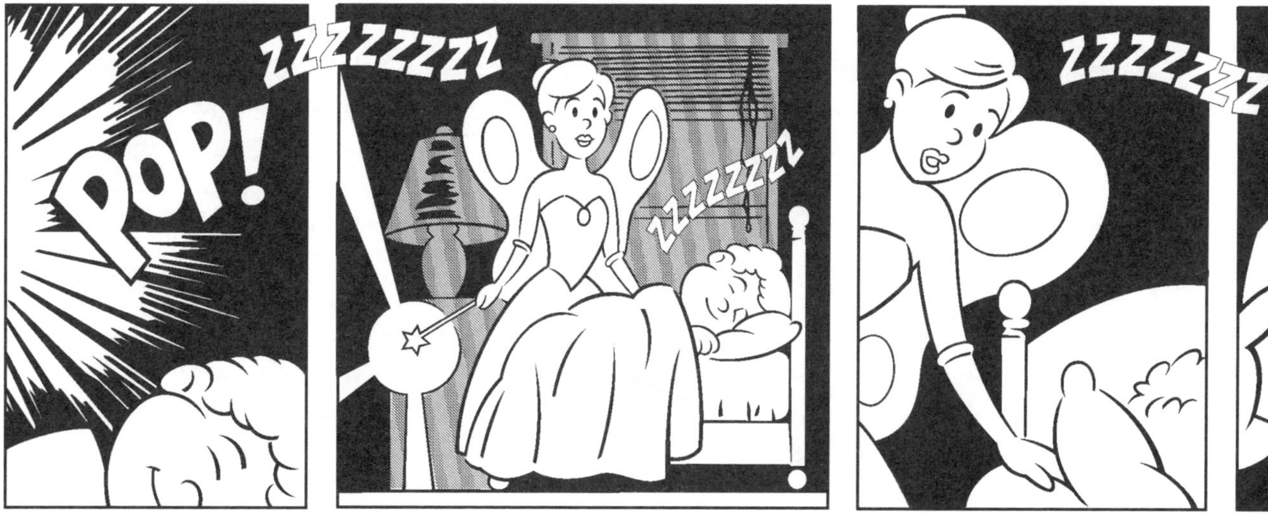
POP!
ZZZZZZZZ
ZZZZZZZ
ZZZZZZZZ
DEAR TOOTH FAIRY,
I'M A LITTLE STRAPPED RIGHT NOW.
CAN YOU ADVANCE THE MONEY ON MY NEXT TOOTH?
THANKS, BOBBY
MURPHY

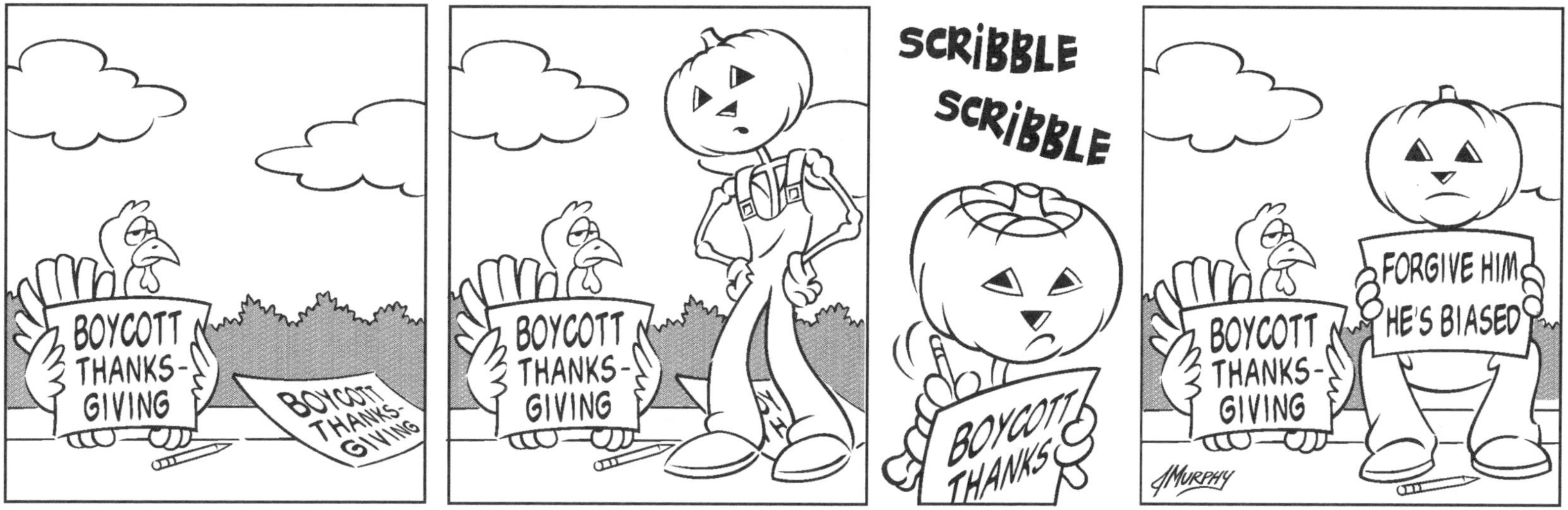
BOYCOTT THANKS-GIVING
BOYCOTT THANKS-GIVING
BOYCOTT THANKS-GIVING
SCRIBBLE
SCRIBBLE
BOYCOTT THANKS
BOYCOTT THANKS-GIVING
FORGIVE HIM HE'S BIASED
MURPHY

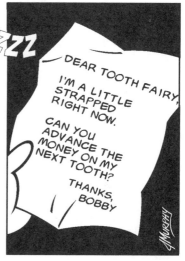

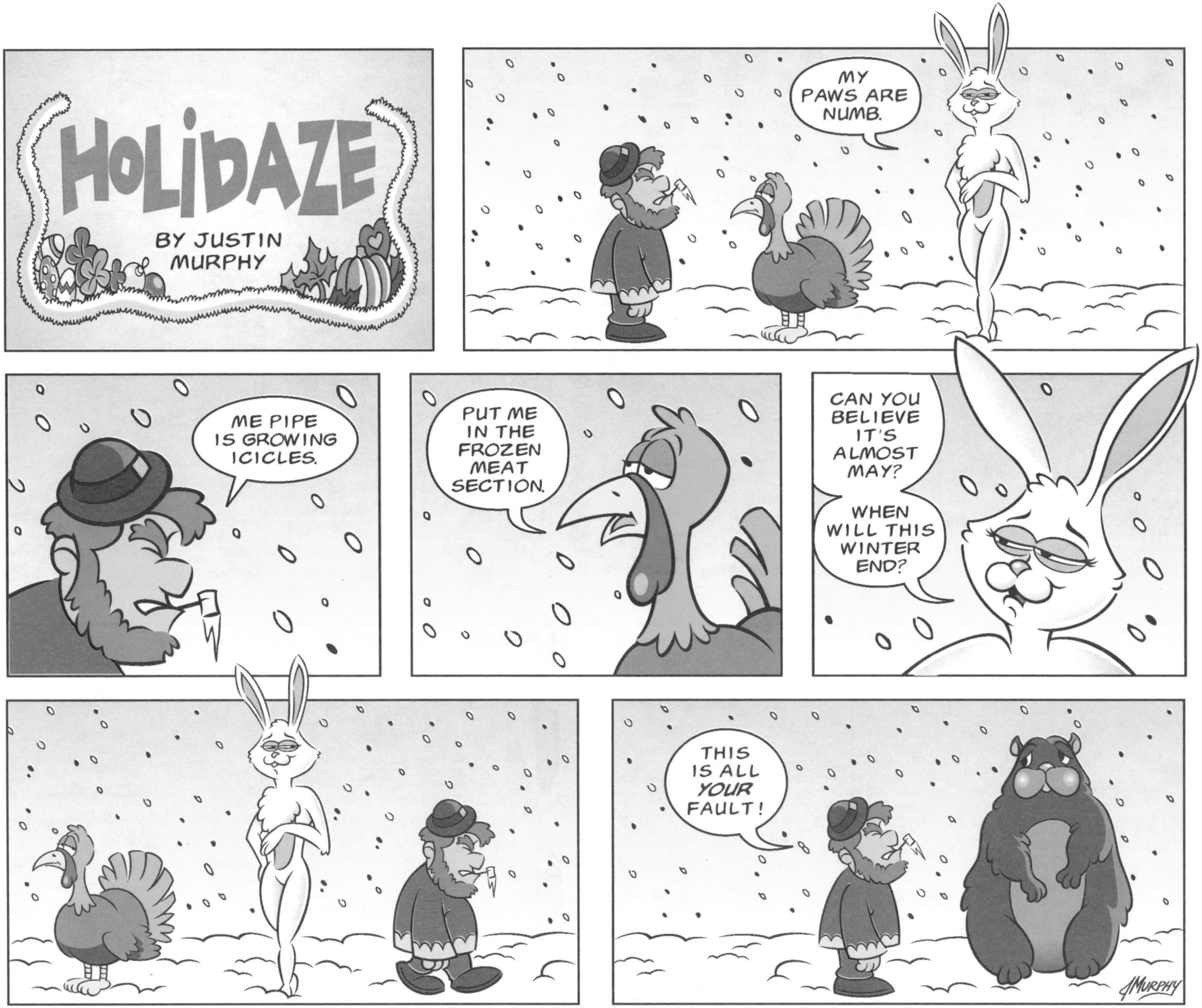
HOLIDAZE
BY JUSTIN MURPHY
MY PAWS ARE NUMB.
ME PIPE IS GROWING ICICLES.
PUT ME IN THE FROZEN MEAT SECTION.
CAN YOU BELIEVE IT'S ALMOST MAY?
WHEN WILL THIS WINTER END?
THIS IS ALL *YOUR* FAULT!
JMURPHY

HOLIDAZE

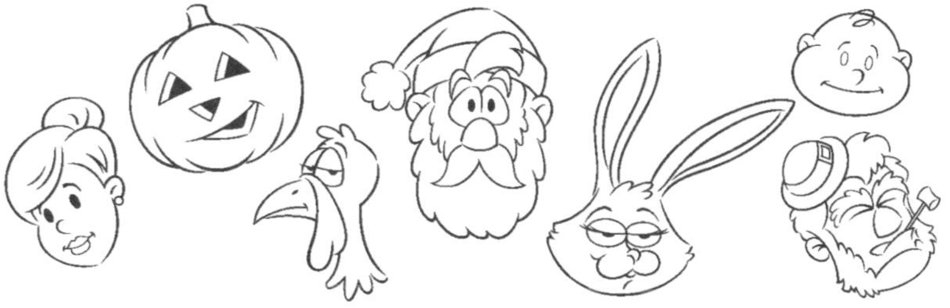

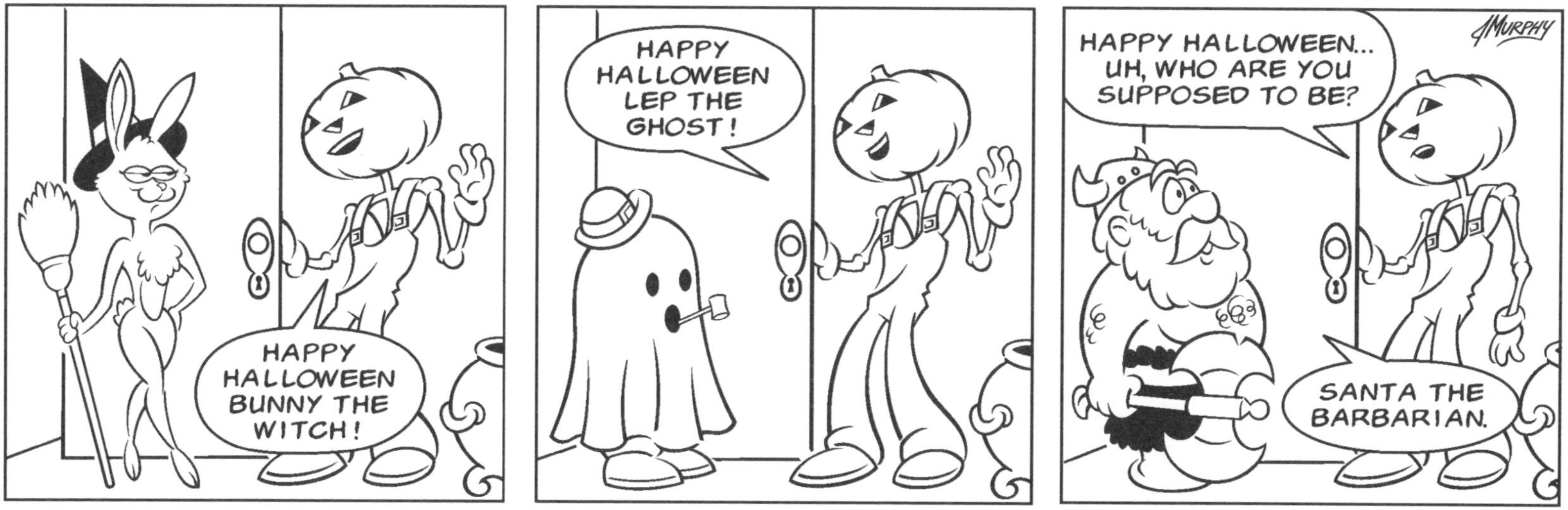
HAPPY HALLOWEEN BUNNY THE WITCH!
HAPPY HALLOWEEN LEP THE GHOST!
HAPPY HALLOWEEN... UH, WHO ARE YOU SUPPOSED TO BE?
SANTA THE BARBARIAN.
J MURPHY

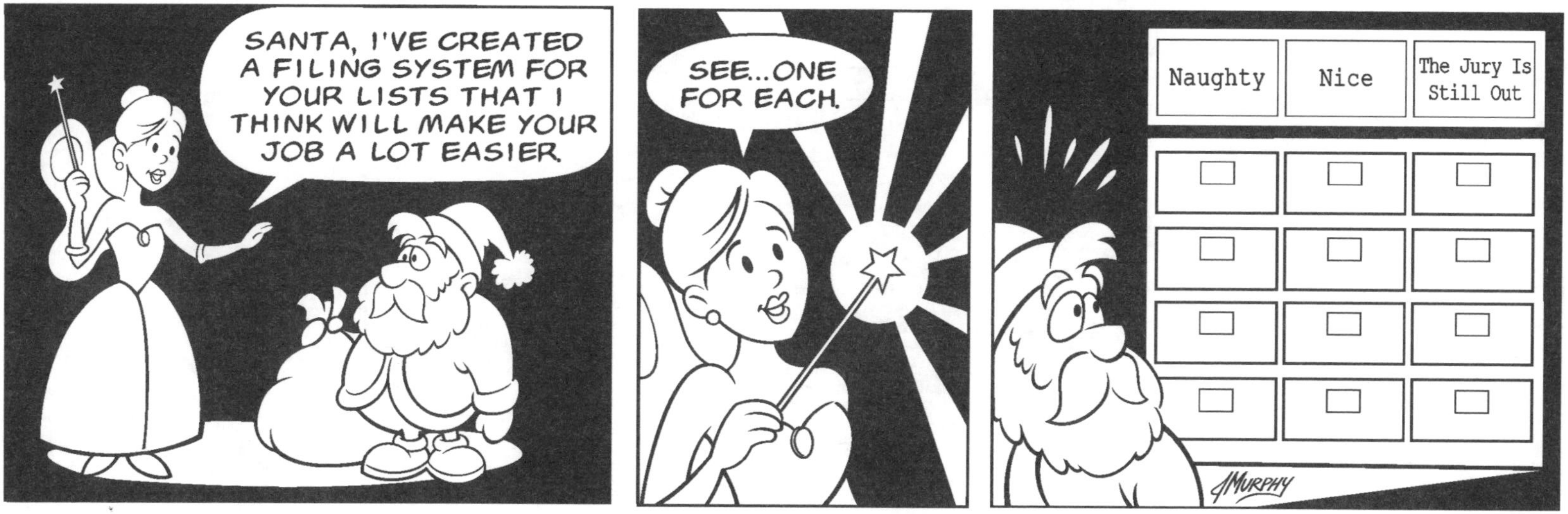
SANTA, I'VE CREATED A FILING SYSTEM FOR YOUR LISTS THAT I THINK WILL MAKE YOUR JOB A LOT EASIER.
SEE...ONE FOR EACH.
Naughty
Nice
The Jury Is Still Out
J MURPHY

HOLIDAZE

IT'S HOPELESS CUPID. I'LL NEVER FIND LOVE. I WORK NIGHTS AND EVERYONE I MEET IS UNDER TWELVE.

HOW CAN I ATTRACT A MAN MY OWN AGE?

SCRATCH SCRIBBLE

SCRATCH SCRATCH

FOR A GOOD TIME LEAVE 50 CENTS UNDER YOUR PILLOW.

LOVE, TOOTH FAIRY

Happy Thanksgiving

TRAITOR

SURVIVAL OF THE FITTEST.

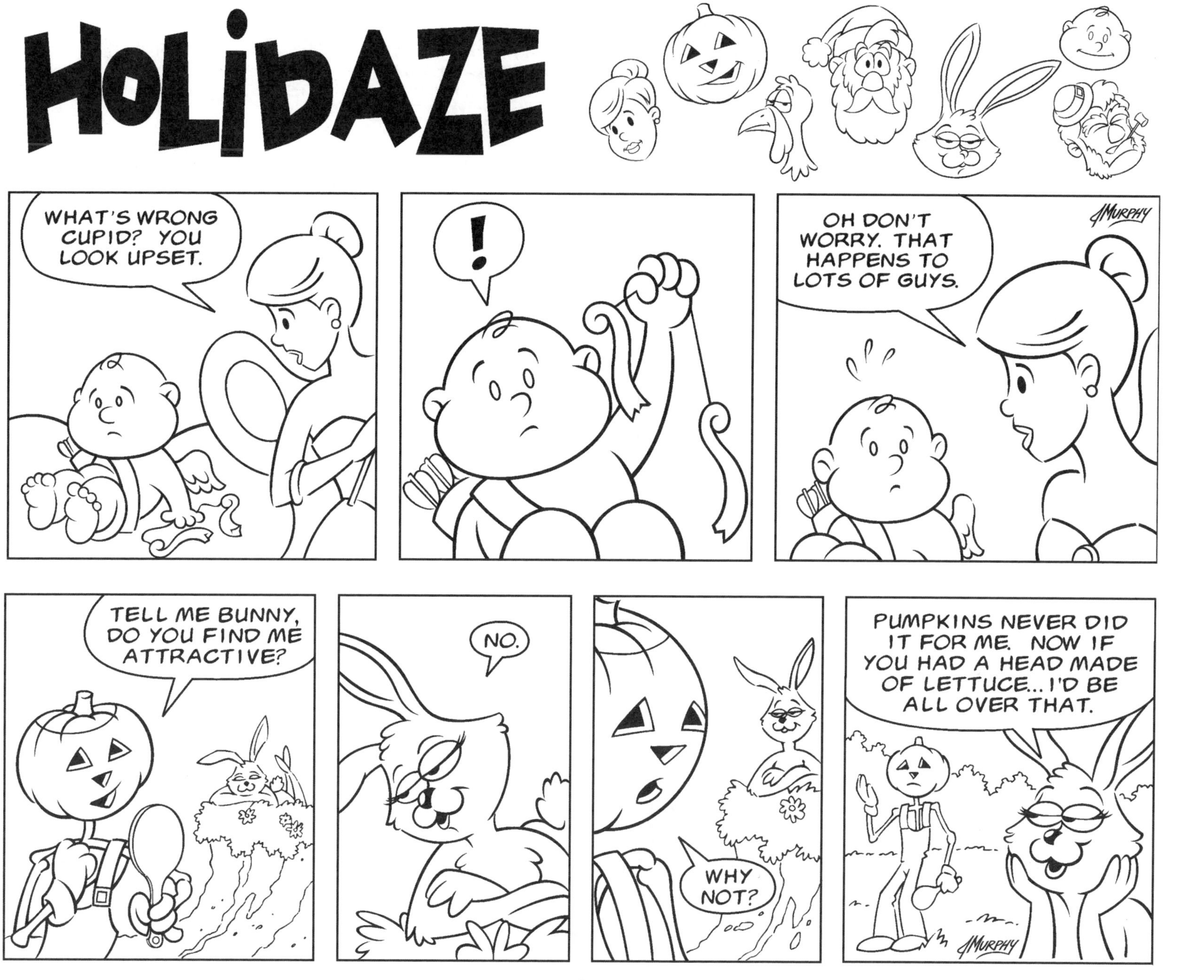
HOLIDAZE
WHAT'S WRONG CUPID? YOU LOOK UPSET.
!
OH DON'T WORRY. THAT HAPPENS TO LOTS OF GUYS.
TELL ME BUNNY, DO YOU FIND ME ATTRACTIVE?
NO.
WHY NOT?
PUMPKINS NEVER DID IT FOR ME. NOW IF YOU HAD A HEAD MADE OF LETTUCE... I'D BE ALL OVER THAT.

HOLIDAZE

BY JUSTIN MURPHY

FATHER TIME, IS IT TRUE THAT BABY NEW YEAR WILL LOOK LIKE YOU IN TWELVE MONTHS?

YES IT IS.

IN TWO MONTHS HE'LL FINISH THE JOYS OF ELEMENTARY SCHOOL, AND ENTER A WORLD OF TEENAGE INSECURITY.

IN FOUR MONTHS HE'LL INCURE HUGE DEBT WHILE IN COLLEGE...

THEN MEET A LOVELY GIRL, WHO HE'LL MARRY AND HAVE THREE KIDS.

IN SIX MONTHS HE'LL CLIMB THE CORPORATE LADDER, ONLY TO FIND THE RUNGS PULLED OUT FROM UNDER HIM...

THEN FACE A DWINDLING RETIREMENT ACCOUNT AND A MESSY DIVORCE.

IN EIGHT MONTHS HE'LL HAVE A MID-LIFE CRISIS, BUY A SPORTS CAR THAT HE CAN'T AFFORD...

AND RE-INVENT HIMSELF BY REMARRYING AND GETTING PLASTIC SURGERY.

IN TEN MONTHS HE'LL FIND A NEW CAREER BAGGING GROCERIES...

AND ATTEMPT TO KEEP HIS GRANDKIDS FROM MAKING THE SAME MISTAKES HE DID.

IN TWELVE MONTHS HE'LL BE STUCK PLAYING BINGO IN AN OLD FOLKS HOME...

FLIRTING WITH TOOTHLESS OLD WOMEN...

AND WISHING HE COULD DO IT ALL AGAIN DIFFERENTLY.

WOW. YOU'RE GONNA HAVE A LOT OF BAGGAGE.

HOLIDAZE

IT LOOKS LIKE ST. PATTY'S DAY WAS A ROUGH ONE THIS YEAR

WHERE ARE YOU GOING LEP?

OFF TO ME CHYL MEETING.

CHYL MEETING?

CAN'T HOLD YOUR LIQUOR.

SALE →

SHOPPING WITH MOM CAN BE SO TRAUMATIC THIS TIME OF YEAR.

HOLiDAZE

CUPID, BEING THE TOOTH FAIRY IS A LONELY JOB. A FAIRY PRINCESS SHOULD HAVE A PRINCE, THEN WE COULD RULE ALL OF **TOOTHLAND** TOGETHER.

WHAT DO YOU SAY? COULD YOU HELP ME OUT?

GIVE ME A PRINCE WORTHY OF CALLING HIMSELF MR TOOTH.

ZAP!

THIS ISN'T WHAT I HAD IN MIND.

J MURPHY

HAVE YOU EATEN A PILGRIM TODAY?

HAVE YOU EATEN A PILGRIM TODAY?

IN THE END IT'S ALL ABOUT SELF-PRESERVATION ISN'T IT?

AYE.

J MURPHY

HOLIDAZE

LOOK AT THE STARS TWINKLING IN THE OCTOBER SKY. ANY MOMENT ALIENS COULD COME DOWN...

AND BRING EVIDENCE OF OTHER LIFE IN THE UNIVERSE!

IT REMINDS ME OF THE GREATEST SCI-FI FILM EVER MADE.

CLOSE ENCOUNTERS OF THE THIRD KIND?

NO SILLY. PLAN 9 FROM OUTER SPACE.

YOU'VE GOT ISSUES.

BOBBY ARE YOU UNDER THERE?

YES.

DON'T YOU WANT TO COME OUT?

I HAVE YOUR MONEY.

GIVE IT TO THE BOOGEYMAN. HE'S IN THE CLOSET.

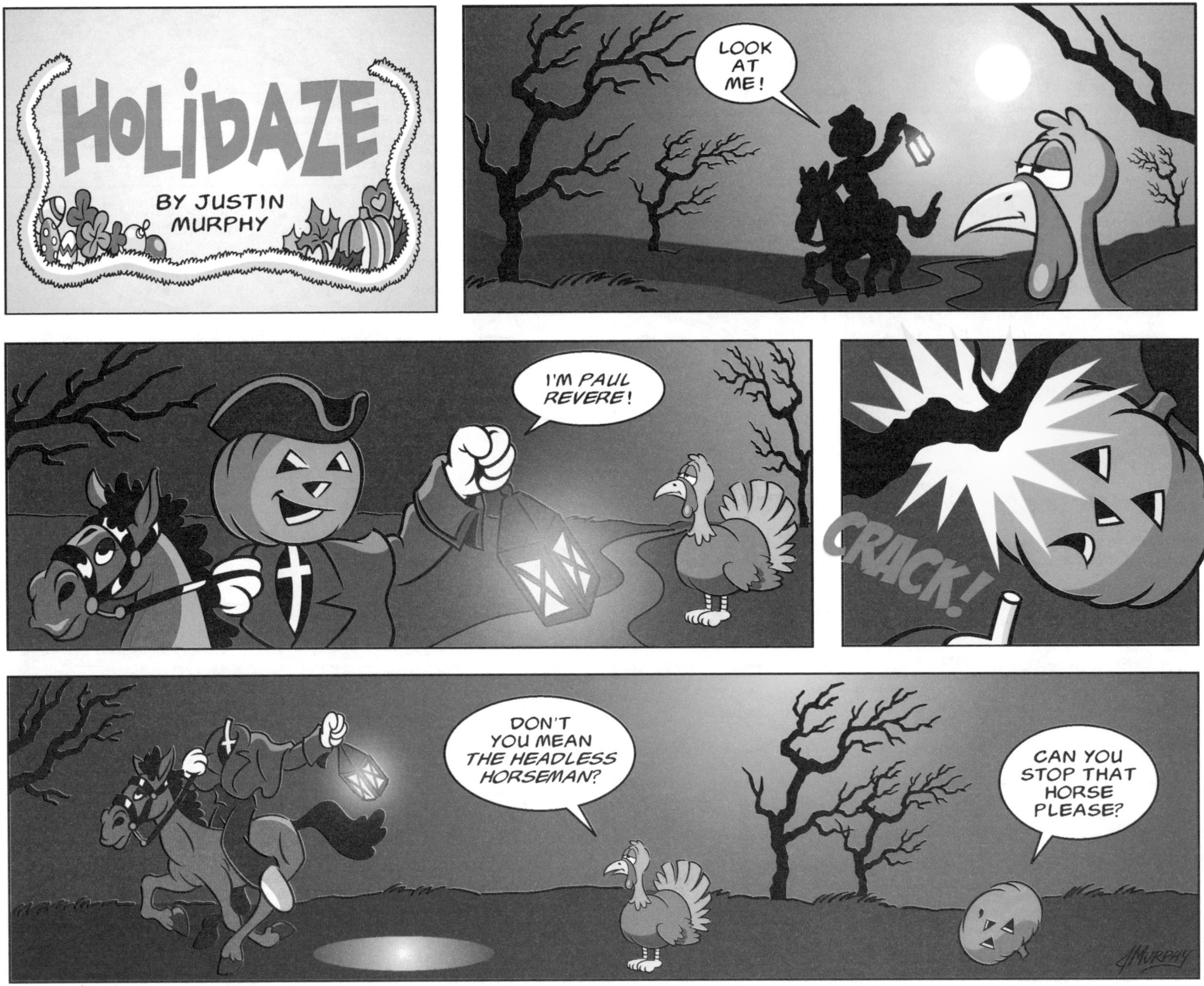
HOLIDAZE
BY JUSTIN MURPHY
LOOK AT ME!
I'M PAUL REVERE!
CRACK!
DON'T YOU MEAN THE HEADLESS HORSEMAN?
CAN YOU STOP THAT HORSE PLEASE?
JMURPHY

HOLIDAZE

THERE'S TOO MANY! JUST TOO MANY!

SANTA WAKE UP!

WHA? OH HELLO BOBBY.

YOU WERE HAVING A BAD DREAM.

WHAT WAS IT ABOUT?

LET'S JUST HOPE CHINA DOESN'T START CELEBRATING CHRISTMAS.

AND NOW WE RETURN TO OUR FEATURE PRESENTATION OF *WATERSHIP DOWN*.

LATER...

WOW. AND I THOUGHT WE HAD IT ROUGH.

MAYBE THEY'LL MAKE ONE ABOUT TURKEYS NEXT.

HOLIDAZE

SANTA WHAT'S WRONG?

CHRISTMAS IS RUINED. I CAN NEVER SHOW MY FACE AGAIN!

IT CAN'T BE THAT BAD. WHAT DID YOU DO?

I SHAVED.

DON'T TRUST HIM. HE JUST WANTS TO EAT ME.

HOLIDAZE

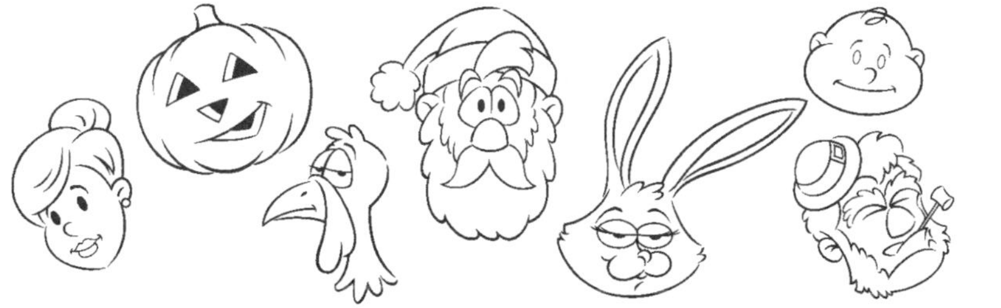

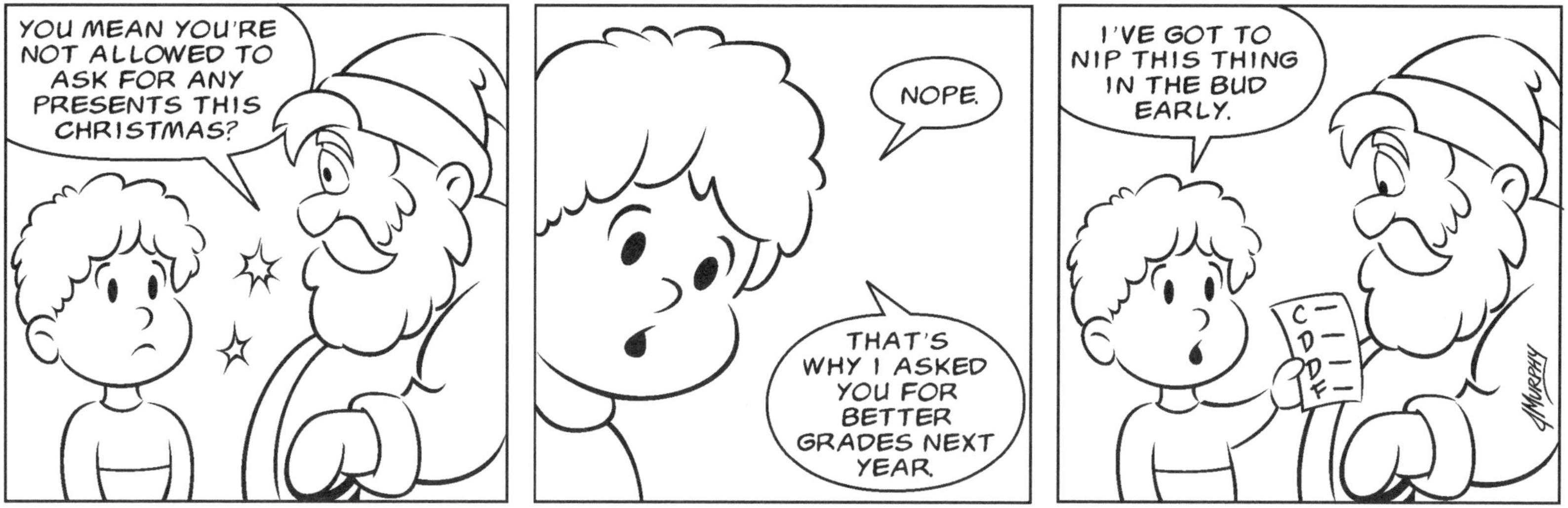

YOU MEAN YOU'RE NOT ALLOWED TO ASK FOR ANY PRESENTS THIS CHRISTMAS?
NOPE.
THAT'S WHY I ASKED YOU FOR BETTER GRADES NEXT YEAR.
I'VE GOT TO NIP THIS THING IN THE BUD EARLY.
C—
D—
D—
F—
MURPHY

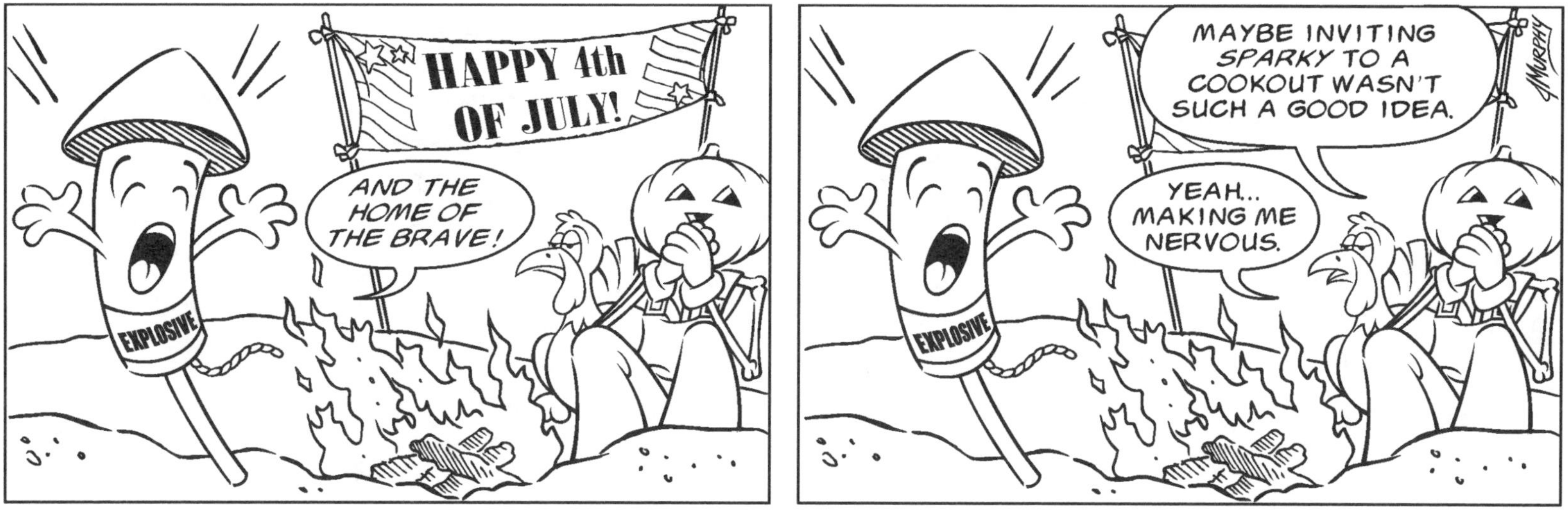

HAPPY 4th OF JULY!
EXPLOSIVE
AND THE HOME OF THE BRAVE!
MURPHY
MAYBE INVITING SPARKY TO A COOKOUT WASN'T SUCH A GOOD IDEA.
YEAH... MAKING ME NERVOUS.
EXPLOSIVE

HOLIDAZE

BY JUSTIN MURPHY

I'M WONDERING LEP. WHAT IS *ST. PATRICK'S DAY* REALLY ALL ABOUT?

GLAD YE ASKED ME THAT, MY BOY.

IT ALL STARTS IN THE YEAR 387 AD....

...BLAH BLAH BLAH...

...BLAH BLAH BLAH...

...AND THAT IS WHAT ST. PADDY'S DAY IS ALL ABOUT.

WOW.

SO WHY DO THEY DYE THE RIVER GREEN?

HOLIDAZE

SOMETHING'S CHANGED.

IT'S MY NEW HAIRSTYLE.

I WAS READING IN A FASHION MAGAZINE THAT CHANGING YOUR HAIR CAN ATTRACT MEN.

THAT EXPLAINS IT.

I CHANGE MINE EVERY DAY.

WHAT'S GOING ON?

AMERICAN IDOL FINALE.

HOLiDAZE

THE CONSPIRACY GROWS.

LEP, YOU REALLY SHOULD GIVE UP THE PIPE.

DON'T YOU KNOW THAT SMOKING IS BAD FOR YOU?

I'M THREE FEET TALL LASSIE.

WHAT'S IT GONNA DO, STUNT MY GROWTH?

HOLIDAZE

WELCOME BACK TO *IRON CHEF AMERICA*!

TODAY'S SECRET INGREDIENT IS... **TURKEY**!

WHY AM I NOT SURPRISED.

THANKSGIVING'S NOT ALL BAD.

THEY EAT OTHER THINGS BESIDES TURKEY YOU KNOW...

LIKE SWEET POTATOES, BUTTER ROLLS, AND CRANBERRY SAUCE...

AND CREAMED CORN, AND GLAZED HAM, AND *PUMPKIN PIE*!

WHAT'S WRONG?

I LOST MY APPETITE.

HOLIDAZE

BY JUSTIN MURPHY

WHAT'S WRONG BOBBY?

I WAS CAROLLING AND MISS MILLER YELLED AT ME.

WERE YOU OFF KEY?

NO, BUT THAT SHOULDN'T MATTER

SHE'S JUST THE MEANEST OLD LADY ON OUR BLOCK.

LET ME GIVE IT A TRY.

♪ JOY TO THE WORLD...

WHAT'S SO JOYFUL ABOUT IT?!

♪ ANGELS WE HAVE HEARD ON HIGH...

ALL I WANT TO HEAR IS QUIET!

♪ GRANDMA GOT RUN OVER BY A REINDEER!

JMURPHY

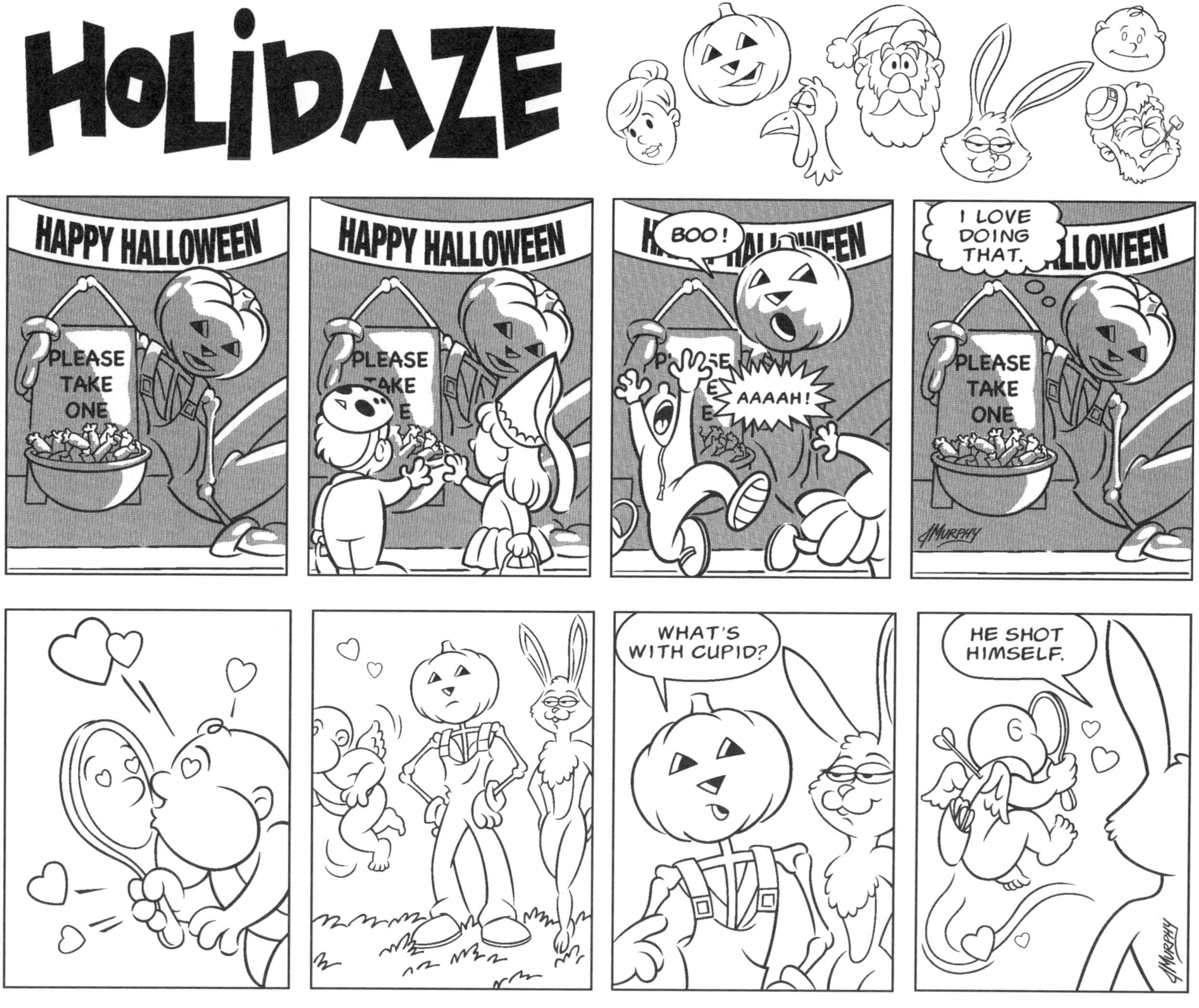
HOLIDAZE
HAPPY HALLOWEEN
PLEASE TAKE ONE
HAPPY HALLOWEEN
BOO!
AAAAH!
I LOVE DOING THAT.
WHAT'S WITH CUPID?
HE SHOT HIMSELF.

HOLIDAZE

JACK.

YES LEP?

BUNNY WANTED ME TA ASK YE WHY YE WHERE SO STUPID?

MMMMM.

I DON'T KNOW. MAYBE IT'S BECAUSE MY BRAINS WERE SCOOPED OUT A LONG TIME AGO.

Pumpkins $10.00

SOMETIMES I FEEL LIKE THERE'S A PRICE ON MY HEAD.

TURKEYS $59.95

YOU HAVE NO IDEA.

HOLIDAZE

COME IN! IT'S OPEN!

BOBBY, IF YOU CAN HEAR ME, I CAN'T ADVANCE YOU ANY MORE MONEY.

IS YOUR TOOTH EVEN LOOSE?

IT WILL BE.

ACLU HEADQUARTERS

ACLU HEADQUARTERS

AC HEADQUARTERS

IN TROUBLE AGAIN HUH?

HOLIDAZE

BY JUSTIN MURPHY

THAT'S THE PROBLEM WITH YOU YOUNGSTERS ON *VETERANS DAY*!

YOU FORGET WHAT US VETS WENT THROUGH SO YOU COULD LIVE IN A FREE COUNTRY AND PLAY YOUR *XBOX*!

ACTUALLY, I HAVE A PLAYSTATION.

DON'T SMART BACK TO ME SONNY,

I'LL BITE YA!

BUT YOU DON'T HAVE ANY TEETH?

THEN I'LL KICK YA!

WITH ONE LEG?

OLD FOLKS SURE ARE RESOURCEFUL.

GRUMPY, BUT RESOURCEFUL.

HOLIDAZE

WOW.

WHAT CAN I SAY? I'M POPULAR

HAPPY MARDI GRAS.

♪ OOOO... I THINK I LOVE YOU, SO WHAT AM I SO AFRAID OF... ♪

I DON'T BELIEVE IT.

A PARTRIDGE IN A PEAR TREE.

THAT'S JUST WEIRD.

HOLIDAZE

WHAT.

I'VE ALWAYS WONDERED WHY THEY WERE CALLED *BEACH BUNNIES*, BUT WHEN I LOOK AT YOU...

SAY NO MORE.

WELCOME BACK TO THE MACY'S THANKSGIVING DAY PARADE..

WILL YOU LOOK AT THAT TURKEY FLOAT? IT LOOKS GOOD ENOUGH TO EAT.

SICK... YOU'RE ALL SICK.

HOLIDAZE

BOBBY, CLEAN UP THIS PIG STY!

BOBBY, TAKE OUT THAT GARBAGE!

TOYS

BOBBY, THE DOG NEEDS A BATH!

NOW I KNOW WHY IT'S CALLED LABOR DAY.

I DON'T GET IT?

WHAT JACK?

THIS CARTOON IS CALLED *HOLIDAZE*, BUT YOU'RE THE *TOOTH FAIRY*.

SO.

SO I DON'T GET IT.

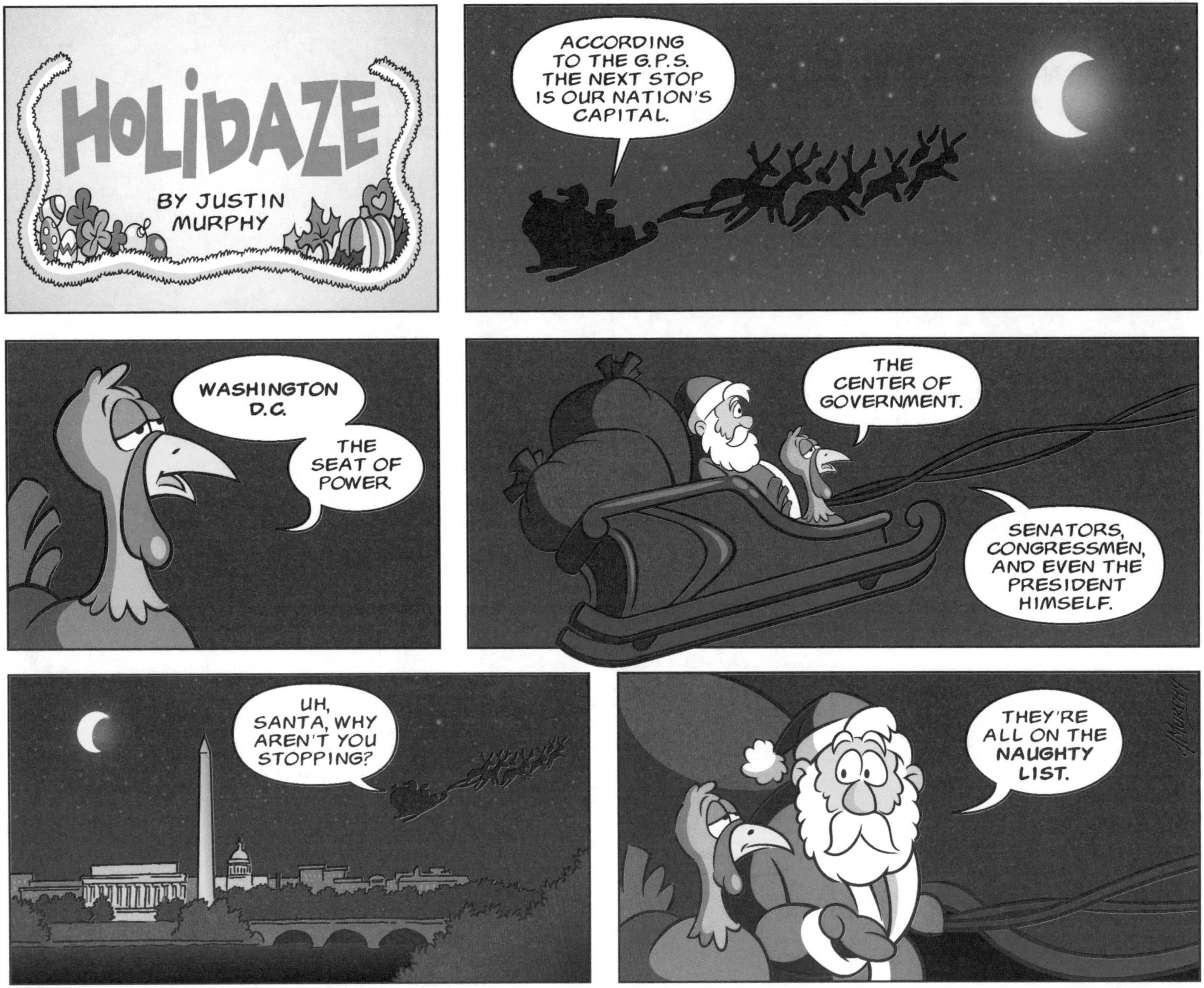
HOLIDAZE
BY JUSTIN MURPHY
ACCORDING TO THE G.P.S. THE NEXT STOP IS OUR NATION'S CAPITAL.
WASHINGTON D.C.
THE SEAT OF POWER.
THE CENTER OF GOVERNMENT.
SENATORS, CONGRESSMEN, AND EVEN THE PRESIDENT HIMSELF.
UH, SANTA, WHY AREN'T YOU STOPPING?
THEY'RE ALL ON THE NAUGHTY LIST.

HOLIDAZE

BUSY FEBRUARY?

ON **MEMORIAL DAY** WE CELEBRATE THE U.S. OF A!

BASTION OF FREEDOM! THE GREATEST NATION IN THE HISTORY OF MANKIND!

BUT SARGE, MY TEACHER SAID THAT THE U.S. IS NO BETTER THAN ANY OTHER COUNTRY...

...AND THAT ALL FORMS OF GOVERNMENT ARE EQUAL.

OH YEAH MAGGOTT!

WELL WHOSE FLAG IS UP THERE WAVING ON THE MOON?!

YOU'VE GOT A POINT.

HOLIDAZE

LOOK! *THRILLER'S* ON!

SOME THINGS NEVER GET OLD.

CUPID, DO YOU KNOW OF ANY NEW PERFUMES? I'VE TRIED EVERY FRAGRANCE ON THE MARKET BUT NOTHING SEEMS TO WORK.

HOW CAN I GET A MAN TO NOTICE ME?

TRY *MAN-CATCHER:* A UNIQUE BLEND OF RED MEAT, MONDAY NIGHT FOOTBALL & BEER

HOLIDAZE

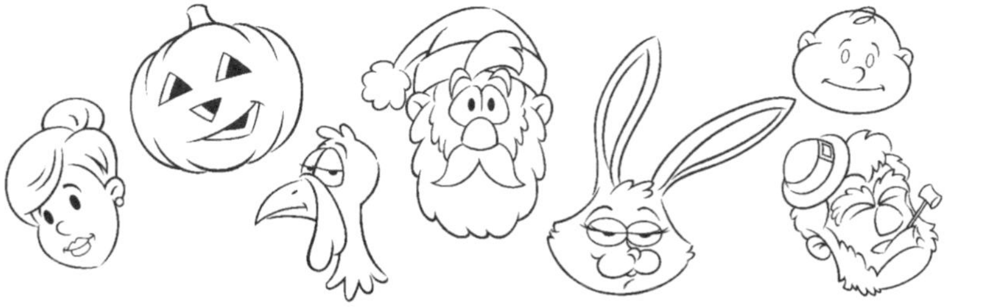

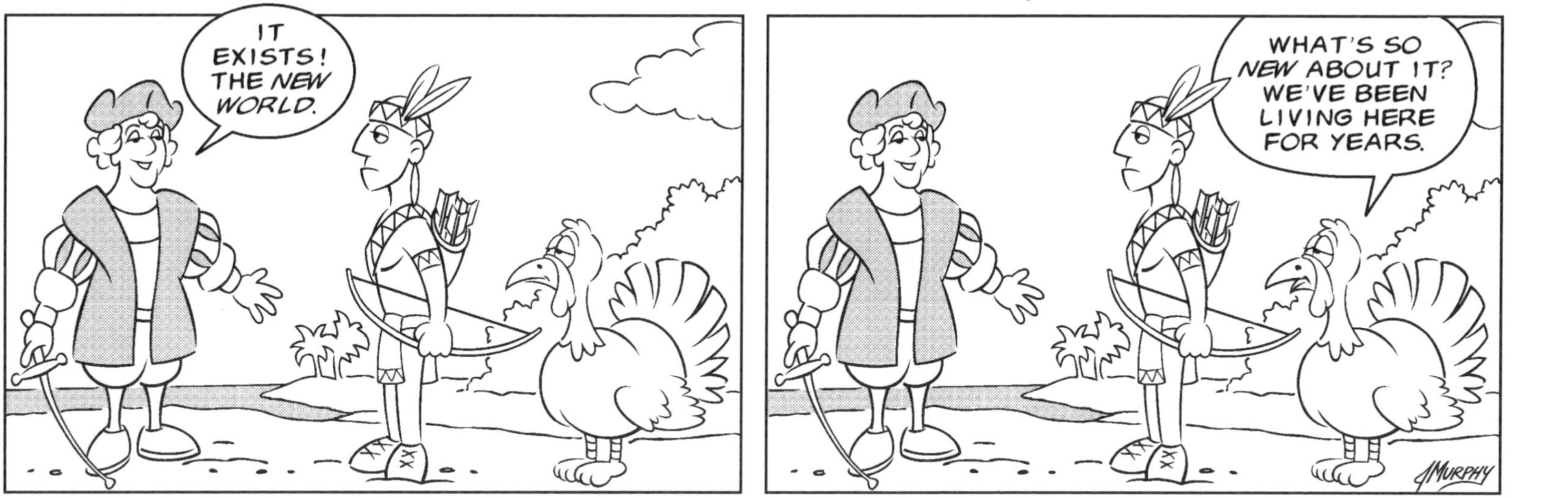
IT EXISTS! THE *NEW* WORLD.
WHAT'S SO *NEW* ABOUT IT? WE'VE BEEN LIVING HERE FOR YEARS.
J MURPHY

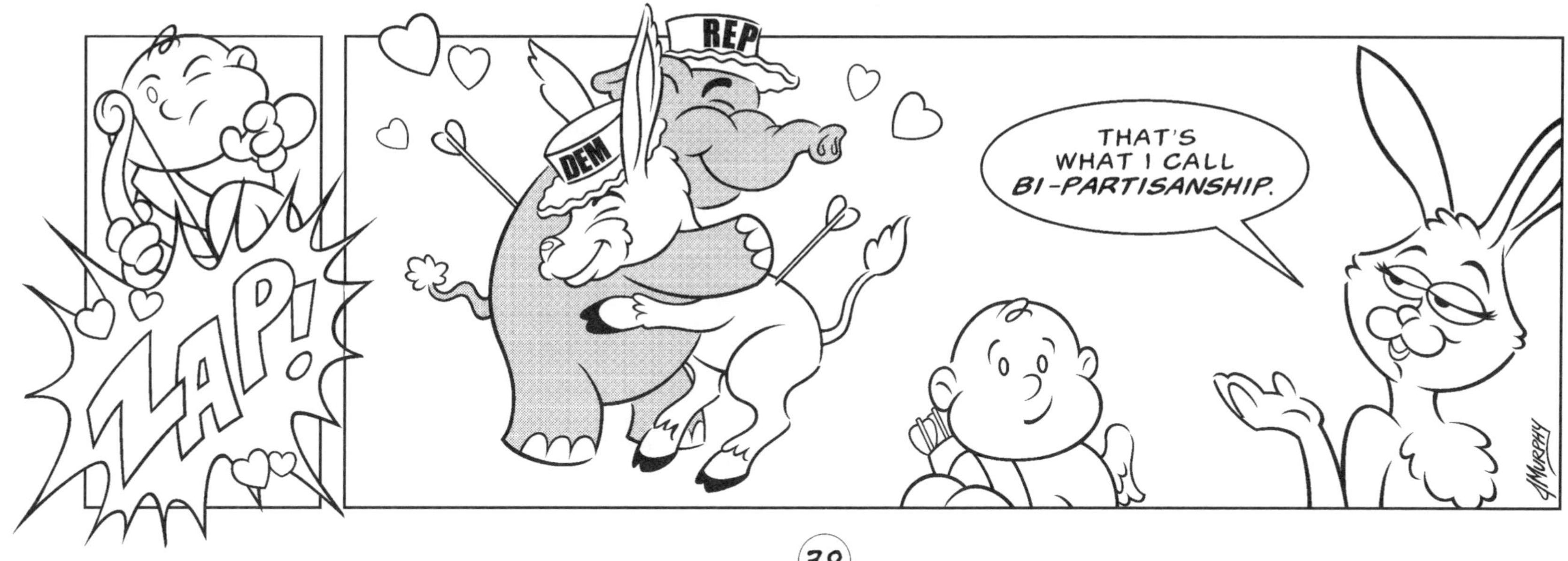
ZAP!
REP
DEM
THAT'S WHAT I CALL *BI-PARTISANSHIP*.
J MURPHY

HOLIDAZE

BY JUSTIN MURPHY

I LOVE COMIC CON!

THE COSTUMES ARE ALWAYS GREAT!

LOOK! HERE COME SOME CLASSIC HORROR MOVIE CHARACTERS!

WOW... AWESOME GLOVE!

OOOO... LOVE THE MASK!

THAT SAW IS A NICE TOUCH!

LEPRECHAUN! I REMEMBER THAT MOVIE!

PERFECT COSTUME!

YOU ALMOST LOOK LIKE THE REAL THING!

I AM THE REAL THING, YOU IDIOT.

CAN WE GO NOW?

I'M UP TO MY BEAK IN GEEK.

HOLIDAZE

WELCOME HOME COWBOY.

DID YOU GET SOME GOOD STUFF?

WE'LL SEE MOM.

KLIK KLAK KLIK KLAK

ALL CANDY IS *NOT* CREATED EQUAL.

YUM

YUCK

BUNNY, HOW ARE WE SUPPOSED TO HUNT FOR *EASTER* EGGS IN THIS?

THE SNOW IS SO THICK, I CAN'T SEE A THING.

WHAT AM I? A RABBIT OR A GROUNDHOG?

I DON'T CONTROL THE WEATHER.

I FOUND SOME!

THEY'RE KIND OF SOFT.

JACK, THOSE AREN'T EGGS!

OOPS. SORRY FAIRY.

GIVING UP, SANTA?

NO BOBBY, JUST RESTING MY BOTTOM ON THIS *LITTLE GNOME* STATUE.

THAT BLASTED GROUNDHOG IS GONNA GET IT.

HOLIDAZE

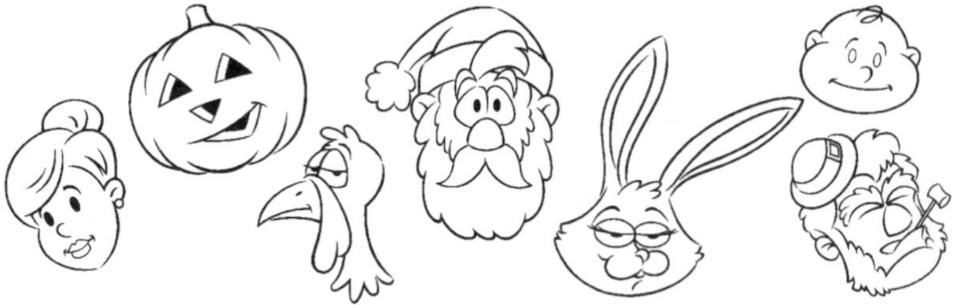

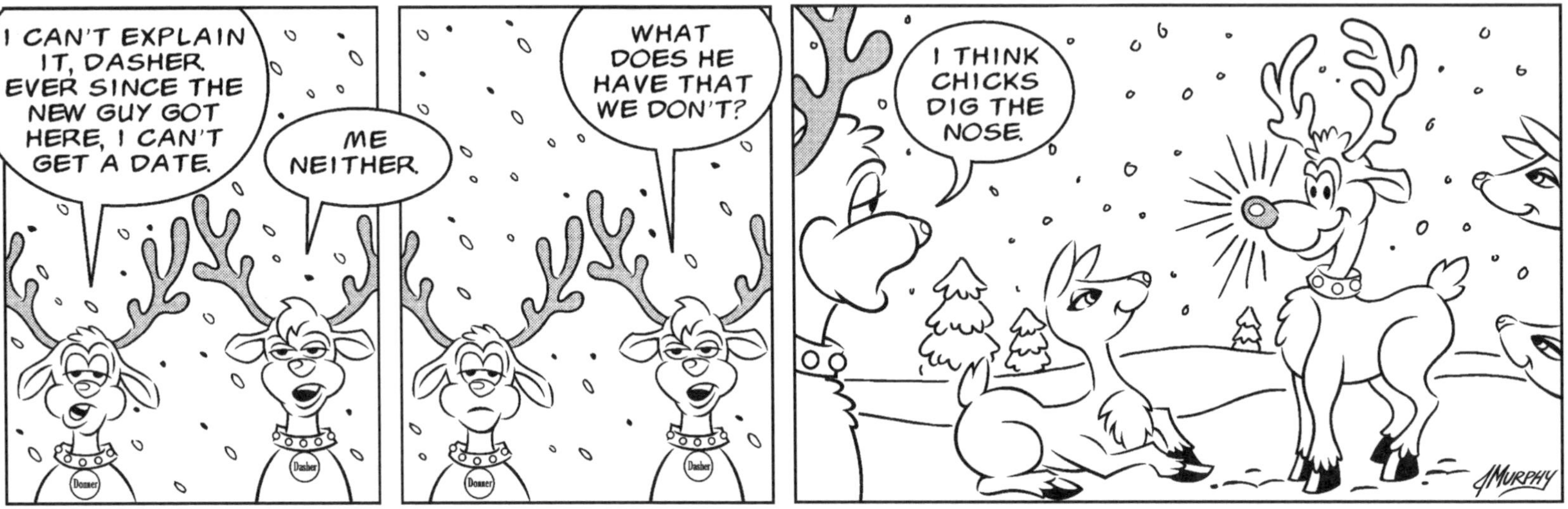
I CAN'T EXPLAIN IT, DASHER. EVER SINCE THE NEW GUY GOT HERE, I CAN'T GET A DATE.
ME NEITHER.
Donner
Dasher
WHAT DOES HE HAVE THAT WE DON'T?
Donner
Dasher
I THINK CHICKS DIG THE NOSE.
J MURPHY

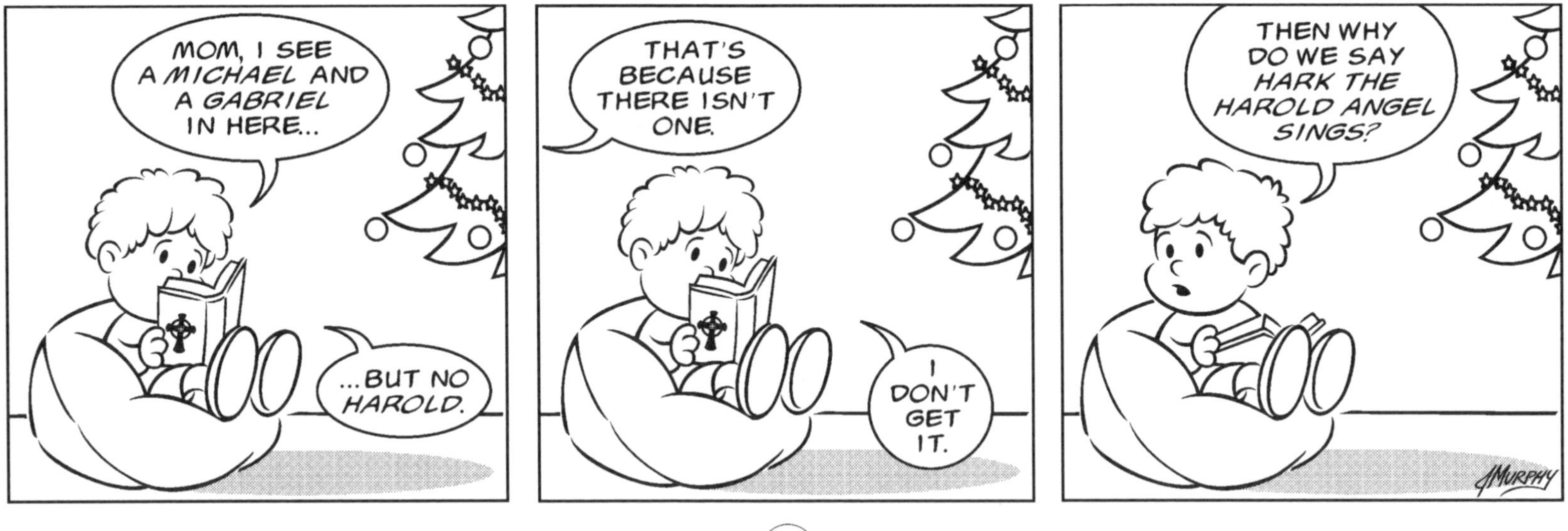
MOM, I SEE A *MICHAEL* AND A *GABRIEL* IN HERE...
...BUT NO *HAROLD.*
THAT'S BECAUSE THERE ISN'T ONE.
I DON'T GET IT.
THEN WHY DO WE SAY *HARK THE HAROLD ANGEL SINGS?*
J MURPHY

HOLIDAZE

HERE AT THE *LINCOLN MEMORIAL* WE PAY TRIBUTE TO OUR SIXTEENTH PRESIDENT.

LINCOLN WAS THE FIRST U.S. PRESIDENT TO PARDON A TURKEY ON THANKSGIVING.

I SEE WHY THEY SAY YOU WERE THE GREATEST.

PATHS OF GLORY! A WORLD WAR ONE CLASSIC. 100,000 CASUALTIES.

PATTON! WORLD WAR TWO. 400,000 LOST IN THAT ONE.

WHAT'S THIS?

SAVING PRIVATE TURKEY.

45,000,000 PER YEAR TOP THAT.

HOLIDAZE

BY JUSTIN MURPHY

44

HOLIDAZE

HEADING TO THE PUB FOR SAINT PADDY'S DAY, EH LEP?

AYE, THAT BE SO, LASSIE.

WHY THE IV?

IT'S FILLED WITH GUINNESS.

HE JUST GETTING A HEAD START.

THANKS FOR HELPING WITH THE CARNIVAL, BUNNY.

I NOW HAVE A RING TOSS, FACE PAINTING AND A DUNKING BOOTH! WHAT ABOUT YOU?

WITH NOVEMBER COMING UP, I HAVE A GAME WITH THE ELECTIONS IN MIND.

REALLY? WHAT'S IT CALLED?

PIN THE LIE ON THE POLITICIAN.

HOLIDAZE

YOU KNOW CUPID, LIFE *REALLY IS* LIKE A BOX OF CHOCOLATES.

AYE, ONE YUM FOR EVERY TEN YUCKS!

BUNNY, I HEARD YOU WERE APPROACHED ABOUT YOUR OWN *REALITY TV SERIES.*

IT'S SURE TO BE A HIT WITH THE *TWENTY-SOMETHINGS.*

REALLY? WHAT IS IT?

THE *BUNNY NEXT DOOR.*

HOLIDAZE

MOM, ELI TOLD ME THAT HE GETS EIGHT NIGHTS OF PRESENTS.

WHY DON'T I?

BECAUSE WE CELEBRATE *CHRISTMAS.* ELI'S FAMILY IS JEWISH, SO THEY CELEBRATE *HANUKKAH.*

HANUKKAH HAS EIGHT DAYS OF GIFT-GIVING AND CHRISTMAS HAS ONE.

WOW. I'M GETTING JIPPED.

HAPPY *MARTIN LUTHER KING* DAY.

I CAN REALLY RELATE TO DR. KING.

YOU KNOW... HAVING A DREAM AND ALL.

HOW'S THAT?

I HAVE A DREAM ALMOST EVERY NIGHT.

YOU AND ME ARE FROLICKING ROMANTICALLY ON THE BEACH...

PLEASE, NOT WHILE I'M EATING.

HOLIDAZE

BY JUSTIN MURPHY

GENERAL WASHINGTON, IT'S AN HONOR, SIR

Hall of Presidents

FIRST OF ALL, *HAPPY BIRTHDAY.*

WE'VE BEEN READING ALL ABOUT YOU IN HISTORY CLASS.

I MUST SAY, I WAS REALLY IMPRESSED BY YOUR CROSSING OF THE DELAWARE.

AND YOUR COMMAND OF THE CONTINENTAL ARMY WAS REALLY SOMETHING.

YOU WERE BRAVE, SELFLESS AND HUMBLE.

I EVEN READ THAT YOU TURNED DOWN THE CHANCE TO BE KING OF THE NEW UNITED STATES.

YOU WERE A MAN OF CHARACTER AND HONESTY. A TRUE PUBLIC SERVANT.

YOUR PRESIDENCY WAS A MODEL FOR ALL FUTURE PRESIDENTS TO FOLLOW.

SO MY QUESTION IS...

WHAT HAPPENED?

HOLIDAZE

AND I WAS HAVING SUCH A GREAT DAY.

FAIRY, IN THESE ECONOMIC TIMES, I NEED A BROADER SOURCE OF INCOME.

COULD YOU HELP ME OUT?

BOBBY, YOU JUST LOST A BABY TOOTH LAST WEEK.

WHAT COULD YOU POSSIBLY HAVE FOR ME NOW?

A JAR OF TOENAILS.

HOLIDAZE

MOM! I'M DONE DECORATING THE TREE!

WHEN I'M BIGGER I'LL BE ABLE TO DO THE OTHER HALF.

I'VE ALWAYS LOVED THE PAINTING OF *WASHINGTON CROSSING THE DELAWARE*...

...BUT I NEVER FELT THEY GOT IT QUITE RIGHT.

NOW THAT'S WHAT I CALL *REVISIONIST HISTORY.*

HOLIDAZE

PREPARE TO FALL TO THE *EASTER EGG HUNT CHAMPION* AGAIN THIS YEAR!

NOT SO FAST. I HAVE SUPERIOR TECHNOLOGY ON MY SIDE.

OH YEAH? WHAT?

AN EGG DETECTOR.

CUPID, MAYBE WE'VE BEEN GOING ABOUT THIS ALL WRONG. THE MAN OF MY DREAMS WILL APPEAR TO ME IN A MAGICAL AND UNUSUAL WAY.

A REAL PRINCE. YOU KNOW, LIKE IN ALL THOSE FAIRY TALES?

SCRATCH SCRIBBLE

SCRATCH SCRATCH

TRY EATING A POISONED APPLE.

IT WORKED FOR SNOW WHITE.

HOLIDAZE

BY JUSTIN MURPHY

MR POLITICIAN. WITH SUCH LOW APPROVAL RATINGS, HOW DO YOU PLAN ON WINNING THIS NEXT ELECTION?

EASY. THE GAME OF POLITICS IS ALL ABOUT *PERCEPTION*, NOT *REALITY*.

THERE ARE A FEW TRICKS THAT ALWAYS WORK TO WIN OVER THE PUBLIC.

ONCE A YEAR I ATTEND A *SPORTING EVENT*, TO SHOW I HAVE ATHLETIC ABILITY.

ONCE A YEAR I ATTEND A CHILDREN'S HOSPITAL BAKE SALE...

...TO SHOW I CARE ABOUT CHILDREN.

ONCE A YEAR I HELP *BUILD A HOUSE*...

...TO SHOW I'M JUST LIKE THE *COMMON MAN*.

HABITAT HOMES

ONCE A YEAR I ATTEND CHURCH...

...TO SHOW I HAVE STRONG RELIGIOUS BELIEFS.

HAPPY EASTER EVERYONE.

♪ WHAT A FRIEND WE HAVE IN JESUS... ♪

HE'S NOT FOOLED.

HOLIDAZE

...O'RE THE LAND OF THE FREEOOEEAH OOAHEEE AND THE HOAHOOOMMME OF THE BRUUAAAVE!

WHATEVER HAPPENED TO JUST *SINGING* THE DARN THING?

IT ALL WENT DOWNHILL AFTER WHITNEY.

ORGANIC COOKIES

SOY MILK

SUGAR FREE

I'LL BE GLAD WHEN THIS HEALTH-CRAZE IS OVER.

IT'S BAD FOR MY WAISTLINE.

HOLiDAZE

I LOVE *STAR TREK.*

IT NEVER FAILS. *RED SHIRT GUY* IS GONNA GET IT.

HE'S DEAD, JIM.

I KNEW IT. RED MEANS DEAD.

I SHOULD TALK TO SANTA ABOUT LOSING THE SUIT.

WOULDN'T WANT HIM TO END UP LIKE THAT *TIM ALLEN* MOVIE.

A RAIN STORM ON *HALLOWEEN* NIGHT.

HOW EXCITING.

THERE'S NOTHING LIKE THE PITTER-PATTER OF RAINDROPS ON A WINDOW PANE.

IT CAN BE QUITE THERAPEUTIC.

BA DOOM

WHO AM I KIDDING? I'M TERRIFIED.

HOLIDAZE

MERRY CHRISTMAS MISTER SCROOGE!

CAN YOU FIND IT IN YOUR HEART TO GIVE?

BAH! HUMBUG!

POW

YOU'LL THANK ME LATER.

SANTA, I DON'T MEAN TO PRY, BUT I SAW YOU FILL THAT SACK WITH PAPER.

WHERE ARE THE TOYS?

WE'RE RUNNING A DEFICIT THIS YEAR,

SO INSTEAD OF GIFTS, I'M SENDING OUT I.O.U.s.

HAS IT COME TO THAT?

LOOKS LIKE IT.

TODAY SANTA CLAUSE, TOMORROW SOCIAL SECURITY.

JMURPHY

HOLIDAZE

BY JUSTIN MURPHY

KEEP YOUR EYES ON THE NUTS.

I'M TRYING.

IT'S JUST A *SHADOW*, LAD.

DON'T LOOK AT IT!

RIGHT.

DON'T GIVE IN!

I'M LOSING STRENGTH.

PHIL! PHIL!!

I CAN'T RESIST.

NOOOOOO

IT LOOKS LIKE WE'LL BE HAVING SIX MORE WEEKS OF WINTER.

YOU DISGUST ME.

HOLIDAZE

Speech: ALL THESE *TEACHER PLANNING DAYS*, WHAT DO YOU SUPPOSE THEY'RE FOR?

WHO CARES? ALL THAT MATTERS IS WE GET THE DAY OFF.

BUT THESE ARE THE PEOPLE WHO HOLD OUR ACADEMIC FUTURES IN THEIR HANDS.

SO.

SO IT SEEMS AWFULLY SUSPICIOUS TO ME.

IN MY DAY, WE DIDN'T HAVE THOSE *RATATAT GUNS*.

IT TOOK TIME TO LOAD A RIFLE.

TEAR

LOAD.

RAM

CAP.

SO HOW MANY SHOTS COULD YOU GET OFF BEFORE THE WAR WAS OVER?

HOLIDAZE

ALRIGHT! *THE LORD OF THE RINGS BLUE-RAY ULTRA DELUXE EDITION COLLECTOR'S BOX SET TRILOGY*!

THANKS MOM!

YOU'RE WELCOME HONEY. THEY'RE PG-13, SO WE'LL HAVE TO WATCH THEM TOGETHER.

LOADED WITH SPECIAL FEATURES AND OVER *120 HOURS* OF *ADDITIONAL FOOTAGE.*

I HOPE YOU HAVE SOME VACATION TIME SAVED UP.

J. MURPHY

Dean of Boys

WHAT ARE YOU IN FOR? WEARING SOME RELIGIOUS T-SHIRT?

NOPE. THIS ONE HAS SANTA CLAUS ON IT.

Dean of Boys

SERIOUSLY?

YEP.

Dean of Boys

(SIGH) PUBLIC SCHOOL.

J. MURPHY

HOLIDAZE

"HUMBUG!" SAID SCROOGE, AND WALKED ACROSS THE ROOM...

"IT'S HUMBUG STILL!" SAID SCROOGE.

MOM, IF SCROOGE HAD SUCH A *HUMBUG* PROBLEM, WHY DIDN'T HE JUST CALL AN EXTERMINATOR?

LEP, I'M ABOUT TO GIVE UP ON LOVE. DO YOU HAVE ANY IDEAS?

WHAT DO *YOU* DO TO FEEL BETTER?

IS THERE A GOOD *IRISH* LOVE SONG YOU COULD TEACH ME?

YOU COULD TRY *WILD IRISH ROSE* OR *LOVE IS TEASING*.

IF THAT DOESN'T WORK, HIT THE BARS, LASSIE.

I KNOW A FEW GOOD *DRINKING SONGS*.

59

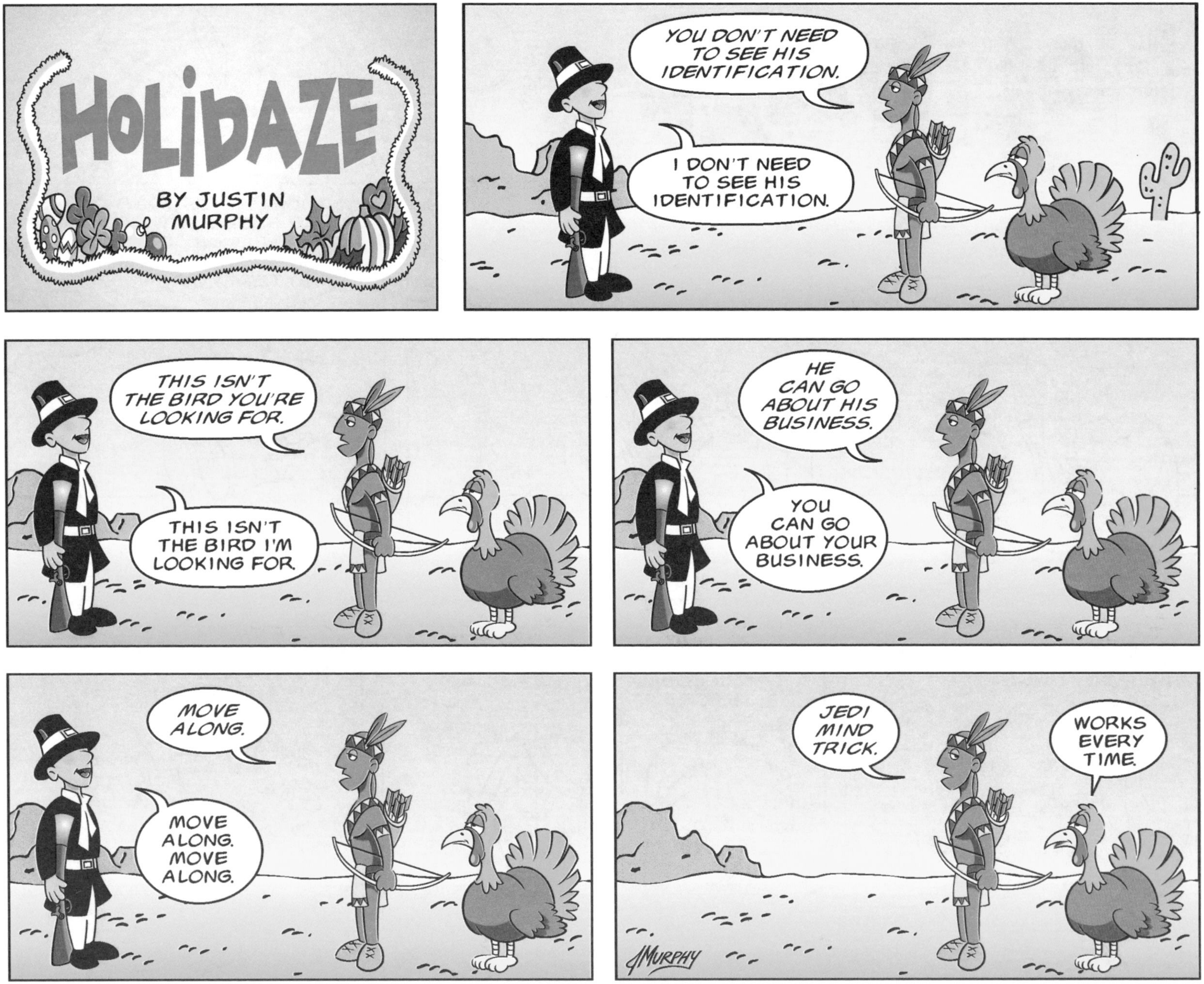
HOLIDAZE
BY JUSTIN MURPHY
YOU DON'T NEED TO SEE HIS IDENTIFICATION.
I DON'T NEED TO SEE HIS IDENTIFICATION.
THIS ISN'T THE BIRD YOU'RE LOOKING FOR.
THIS ISN'T THE BIRD I'M LOOKING FOR.
HE CAN GO ABOUT HIS BUSINESS.
YOU CAN GO ABOUT YOUR BUSINESS.
MOVE ALONG.
MOVE ALONG. MOVE ALONG.
JEDI MIND TRICK.
WORKS EVERY TIME.
J MURPHY

HOLIDAZE

MENNY, WHAT DO KIDS LIKE TO DO ON HANUKKAH?

NUN! GIMEL! HAY! SHUN!

🎵 YOU SPIN ME RIGHT ROUND BABY, RIGHT ROUND, LIKE A **DREIDEL**, BABY, RIGHT ROUND, ROUND ROUND... 🎵

PRETTY COOL.

FABREGÉ EGGS ARE RARE AND PRICELESS.

WOW. SO DON'T THE *REGULAR* EGGS GET JEALOUS?

SURE. THEY PLAY THE SAME GAME THAT HUMANS DO.

WHAT'S THAT?

CLASS WARFARE.

HOLIDAZE

IF I GO AS *HARRY POTTER*, KYLE WILL BE MAD CAUSE *HE'S* GOING AS HARRY.

IF I GO AS A *JEDI*, MARK WILL BE MAD 'CAUSE *HE'S* GOING AS A JEDI.

COSTUMES

WHAT'S *THAT* SUPPOSED TO BE?

A GHOST.

IT'S THE LAMEST THING IN THE BOOK.

WHY IS IT WHEN YOU TRY TO PLEASE *EVERYBODY* YOU END UP PLEASING *NOBODY*?

WHAT A HAUNTED HOUSE, EH BUNNY?

WE'VE SEEN *GHOSTS* AND *SPIRITS* OF EVERY KIND.

BANG! BANG!

SOMEONE'S AT THE DOOR

CREAK!

GOOD EVENING.

I'M RUNNING FOR OFFICE AND I NEED YOUR VOTE.

JACK!

ADD *VAMPIRES* TO YOUR LIST.

HOLIDAZE

POP!

ZZZZZZZ

ZZZZZZZ

ZZZZZZZ

DEAR TOOTH FAIRY,

IF YOU'RE STILL LOOKING FOR A MAN IN 10 YEARS, I'LL BE LEGAL AND AVAILABLE.

XOXO BOBBY

FIRE! FIRE! LOOK, I JUST BLEW HIS HEAD OFF!

BLAM BLAM BLAM BA-DOOM

THAT'S THE ANNIHILATOR! IT VAPORIZES EVERYTHING ON THE SCREEN!

IS *THIS* WHAT I DELIVERED TO ALL THE KIDS LAST YEAR?

ONE THING'S FOR SURE... IT AIN'T CANDYLAND.

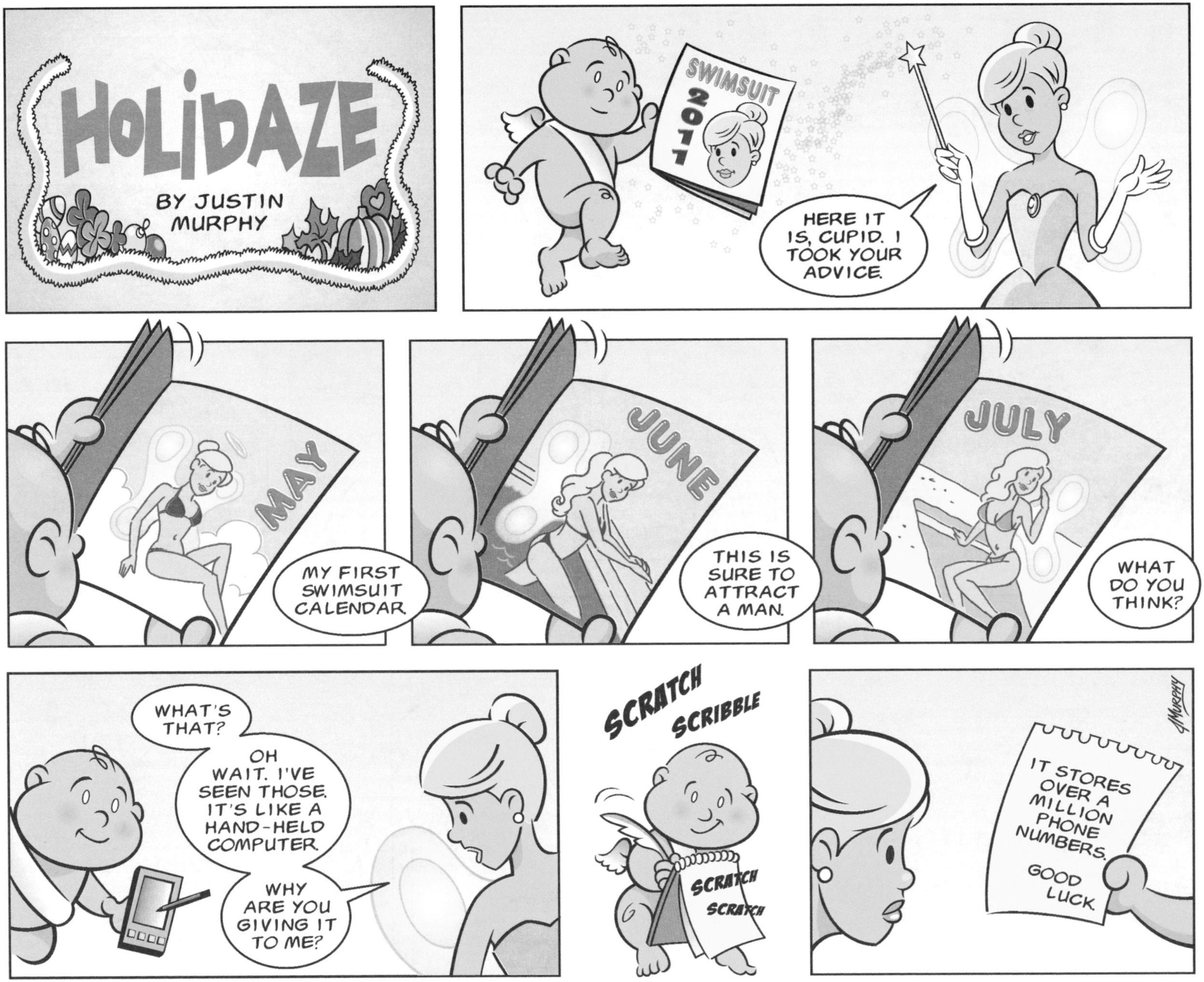
HOLIDAZE
BY JUSTIN MURPHY
SWIMSUIT 2011
HERE IT IS, CUPID. I TOOK YOUR ADVICE.
MAY
MY FIRST SWIMSUIT CALENDAR.
JUNE
THIS IS SURE TO ATTRACT A MAN.
JULY
WHAT DO YOU THINK?
WHAT'S THAT?
OH WAIT. I'VE SEEN THOSE. IT'S LIKE A HAND-HELD COMPUTER.
WHY ARE YOU GIVING IT TO ME?
SCRATCH
SCRIBBLE
SCRATCH
SCRATCH
J MURPHY
IT STORES OVER A MILLION PHONE NUMBERS.
GOOD LUCK.

HOLIDAZE

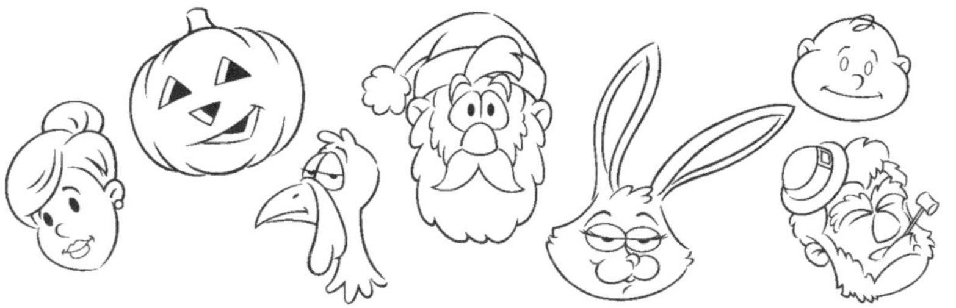

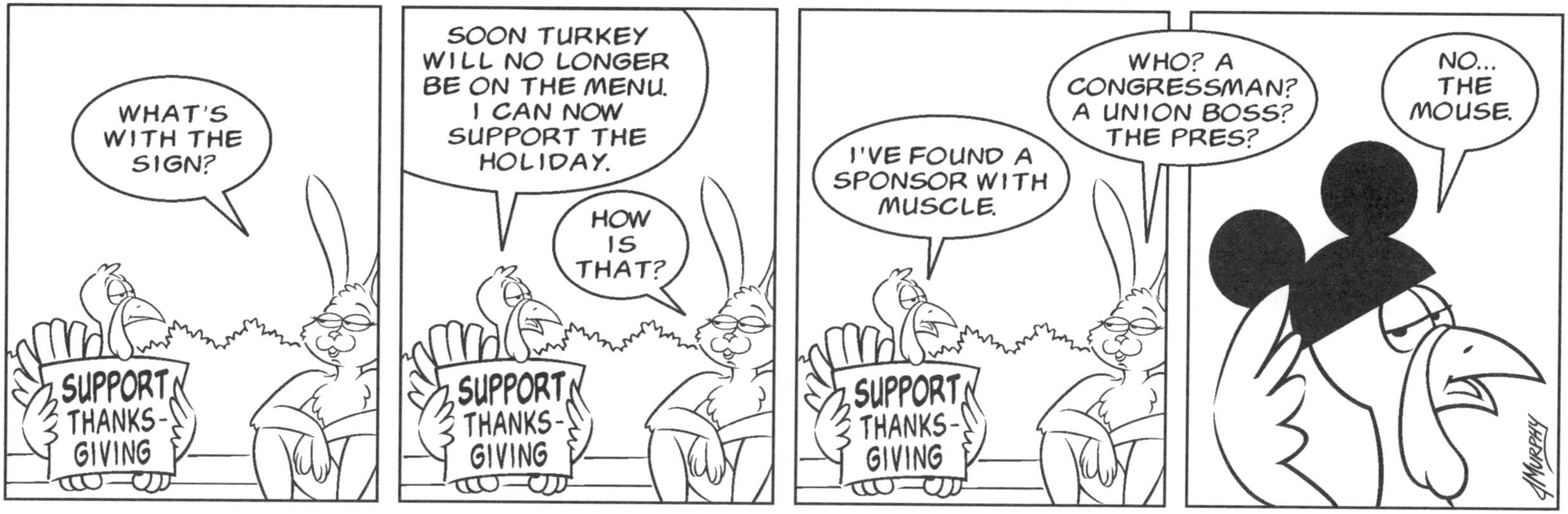

WHAT'S WITH THE SIGN?
SUPPORT THANKS-GIVING
SOON TURKEY WILL NO LONGER BE ON THE MENU. I CAN NOW SUPPORT THE HOLIDAY.
SUPPORT THANKS-GIVING
HOW IS THAT?
I'VE FOUND A SPONSOR WITH MUSCLE.
SUPPORT THANKS-GIVING
WHO? A CONGRESSMAN? A UNION BOSS? THE PRES?
NO... THE MOUSE.
MURPHY

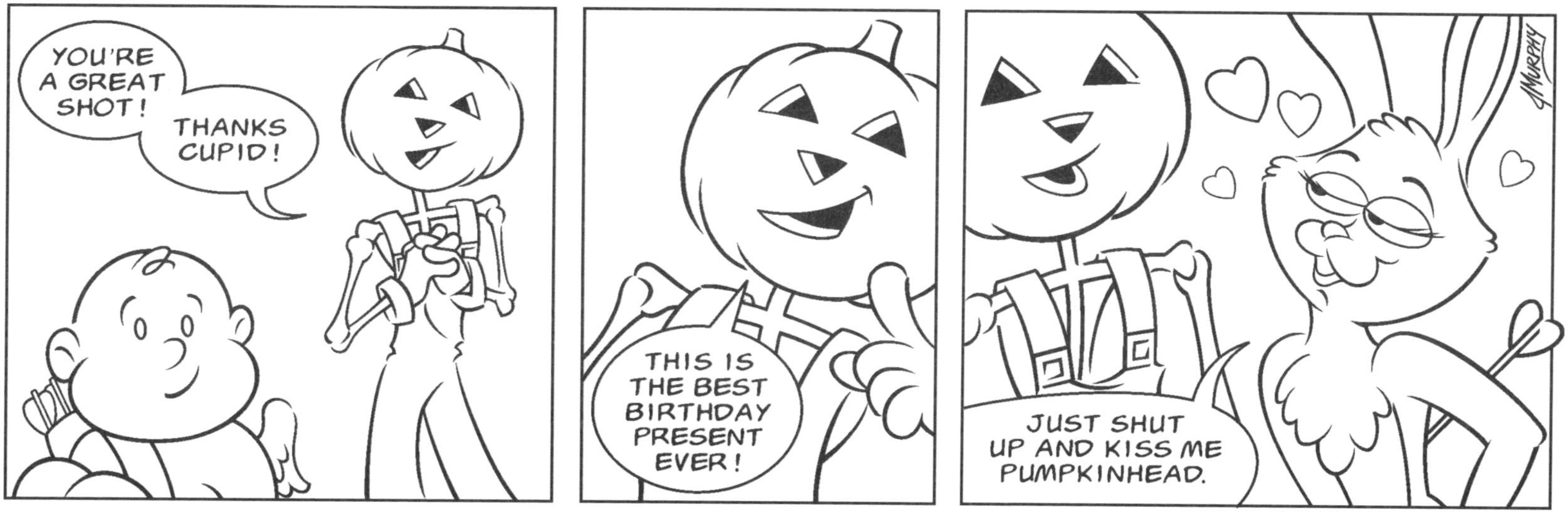

YOU'RE A GREAT SHOT!
THANKS CUPID!
THIS IS THE BEST BIRTHDAY PRESENT EVER!
MURPHY
JUST SHUT UP AND KISS ME PUMPKINHEAD.

HOLIDAZE

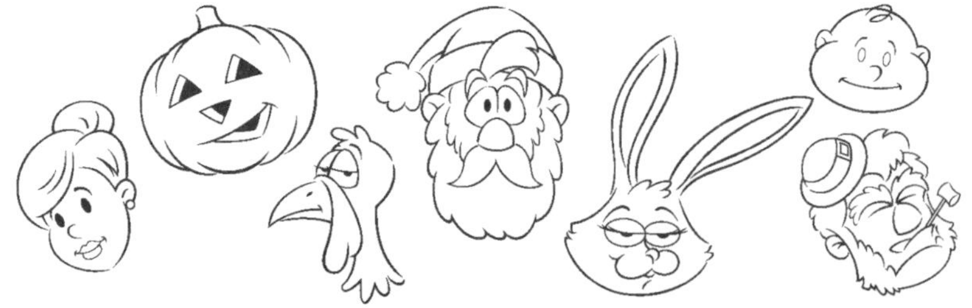

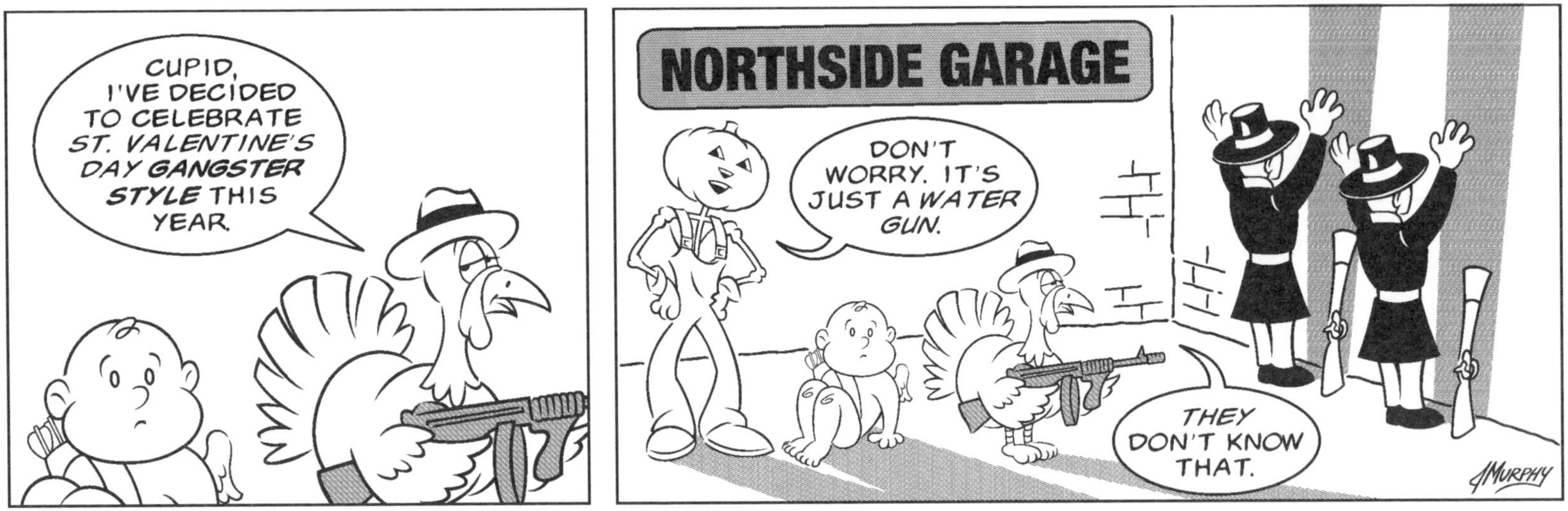
CUPID, I'VE DECIDED TO CELEBRATE *ST. VALENTINE'S DAY* ***GANGSTER STYLE*** THIS YEAR.
NORTHSIDE GARAGE
DON'T WORRY. IT'S JUST A *WATER GUN.*
THEY DON'T KNOW THAT.

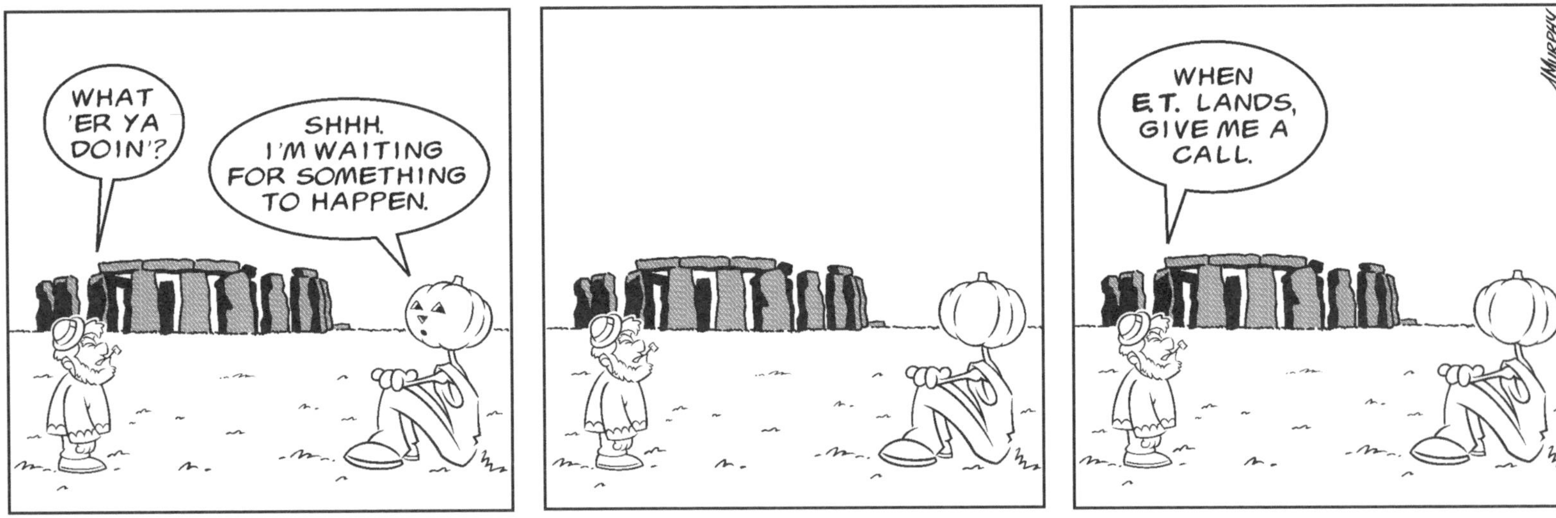
WHAT 'ER YA DOIN'?
SHHH. I'M WAITING FOR SOMETHING TO HAPPEN.
WHEN **E.T.** LANDS, GIVE ME A CALL.

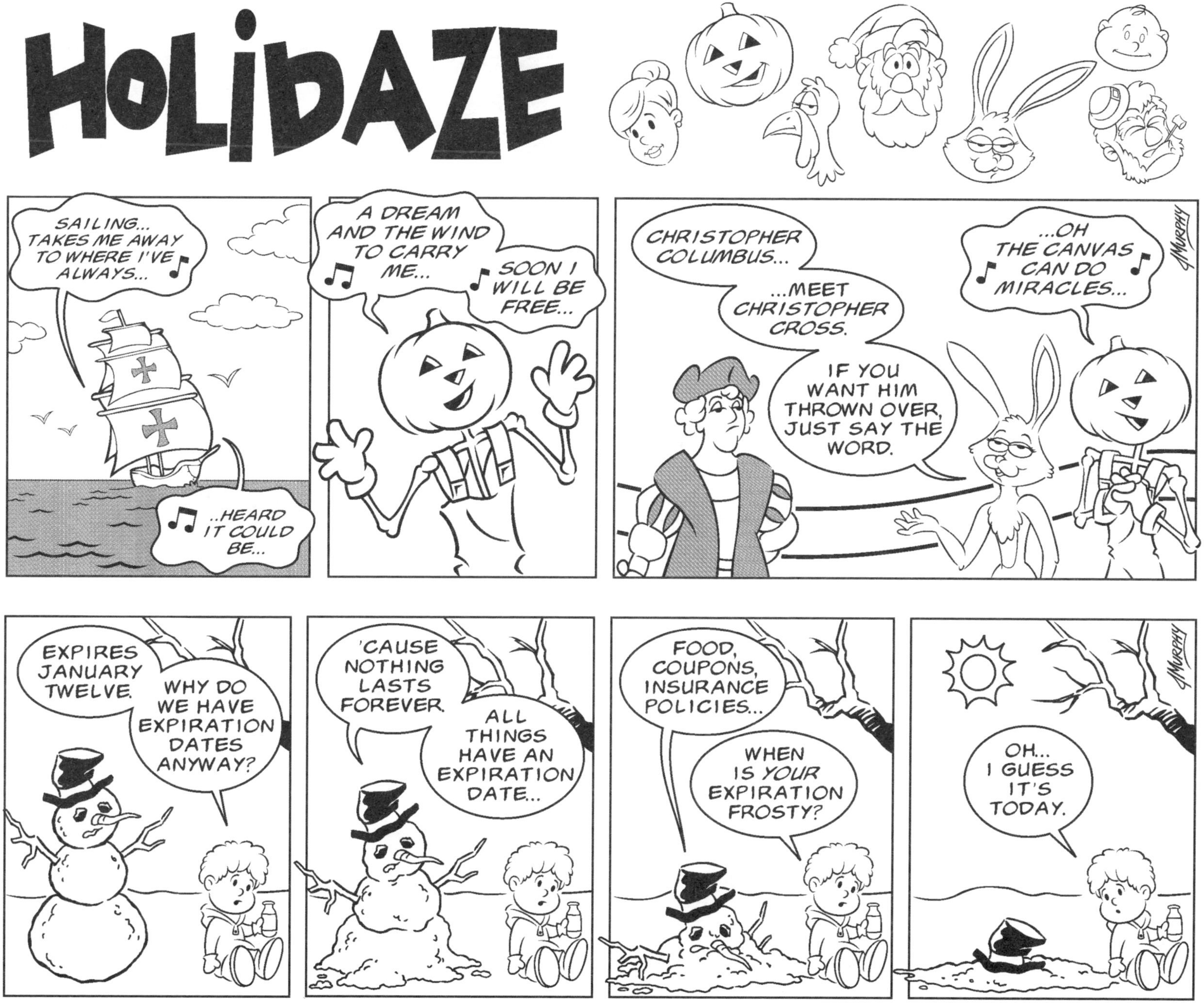
HOLIDAZE
SAILING... TAKES ME AWAY TO WHERE I'VE ALWAYS...
..HEARD IT COULD BE...
A DREAM AND THE WIND TO CARRY ME...
SOON I WILL BE FREE...
CHRISTOPHER COLUMBUS...
...MEET CHRISTOPHER CROSS.
IF YOU WANT HIM THROWN OVER, JUST SAY THE WORD.
...OH THE CANVAS CAN DO MIRACLES...
MURPHY
EXPIRES JANUARY TWELVE.
WHY DO WE HAVE EXPIRATION DATES ANYWAY?
'CAUSE NOTHING LASTS FOREVER.
ALL THINGS HAVE AN EXPIRATION DATE...
FOOD, COUPONS, INSURANCE POLICIES...
WHEN IS *YOUR* EXPIRATION FROSTY?
OH... I GUESS IT'S TODAY.
MURPHY

HOLIDAZE

BY JUSTIN MURPHY

IT'S ST. PATRICK'S DAY, LEP.

WHY AREN'T YOU GOING GREEN?

GO GREEN! GO GREEN! I'M SICK OF HEARIN' IT!

WEARING GREEN USED TO BE ABOUT IRISH HERITAGE AND NOTHING ELSE!

I'LL NOT BE PART OF ANYONE'S POLITICAL AGENDA!

AYE, WHAT IS IT, SARGE?

RED?! YOU TURNED COMMIE ON US?

I GIVE UP.

HOLIDAZE

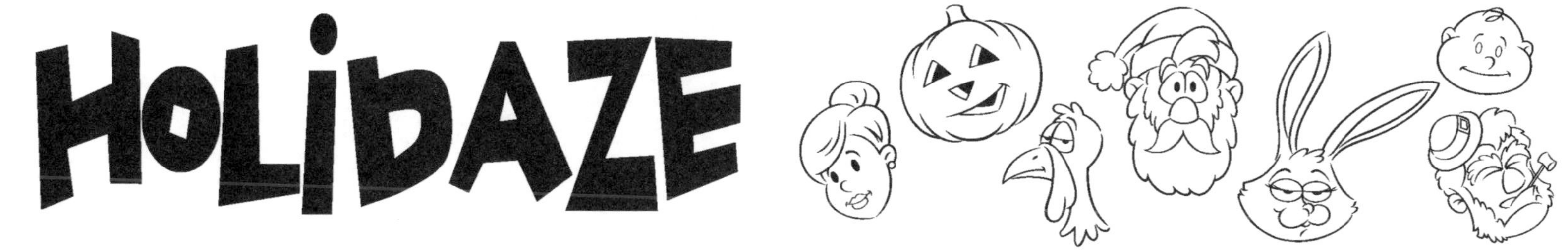

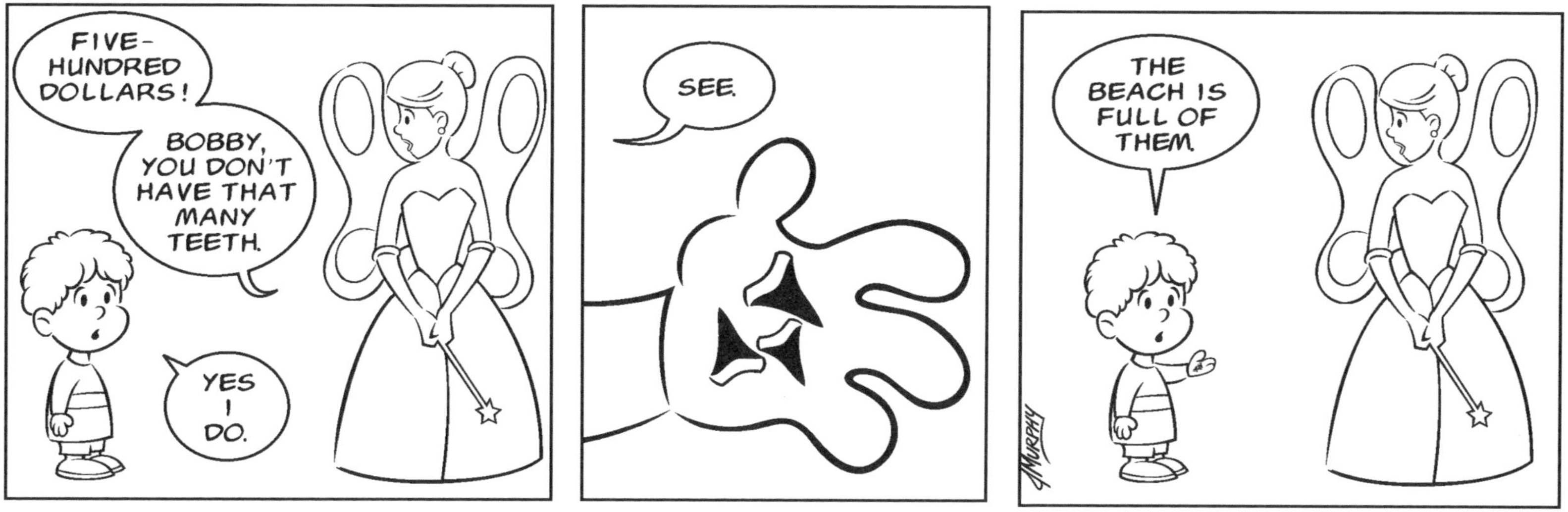
FIVE-HUNDRED DOLLARS!
BOBBY, YOU DON'T HAVE THAT MANY TEETH.
YES I DO.
SEE.
THE BEACH IS FULL OF THEM.

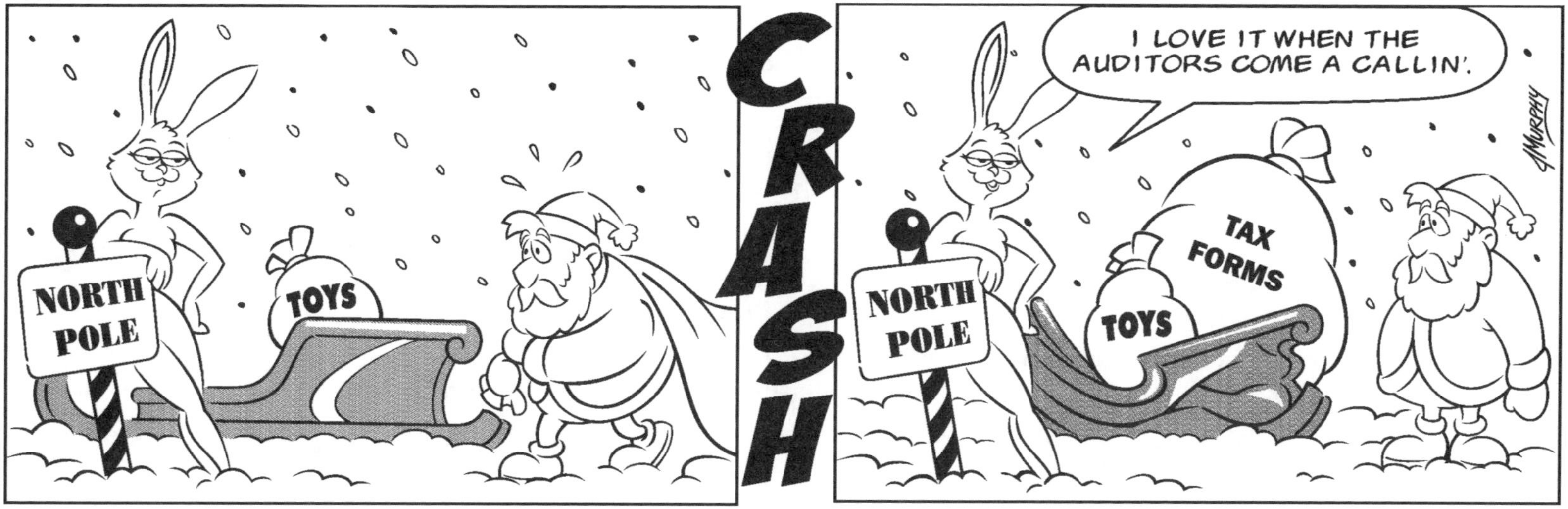
NORTH POLE
TOYS
CRASH
I LOVE IT WHEN THE AUDITORS COME A CALLIN'.
NORTH POLE
TAX FORMS
TOYS

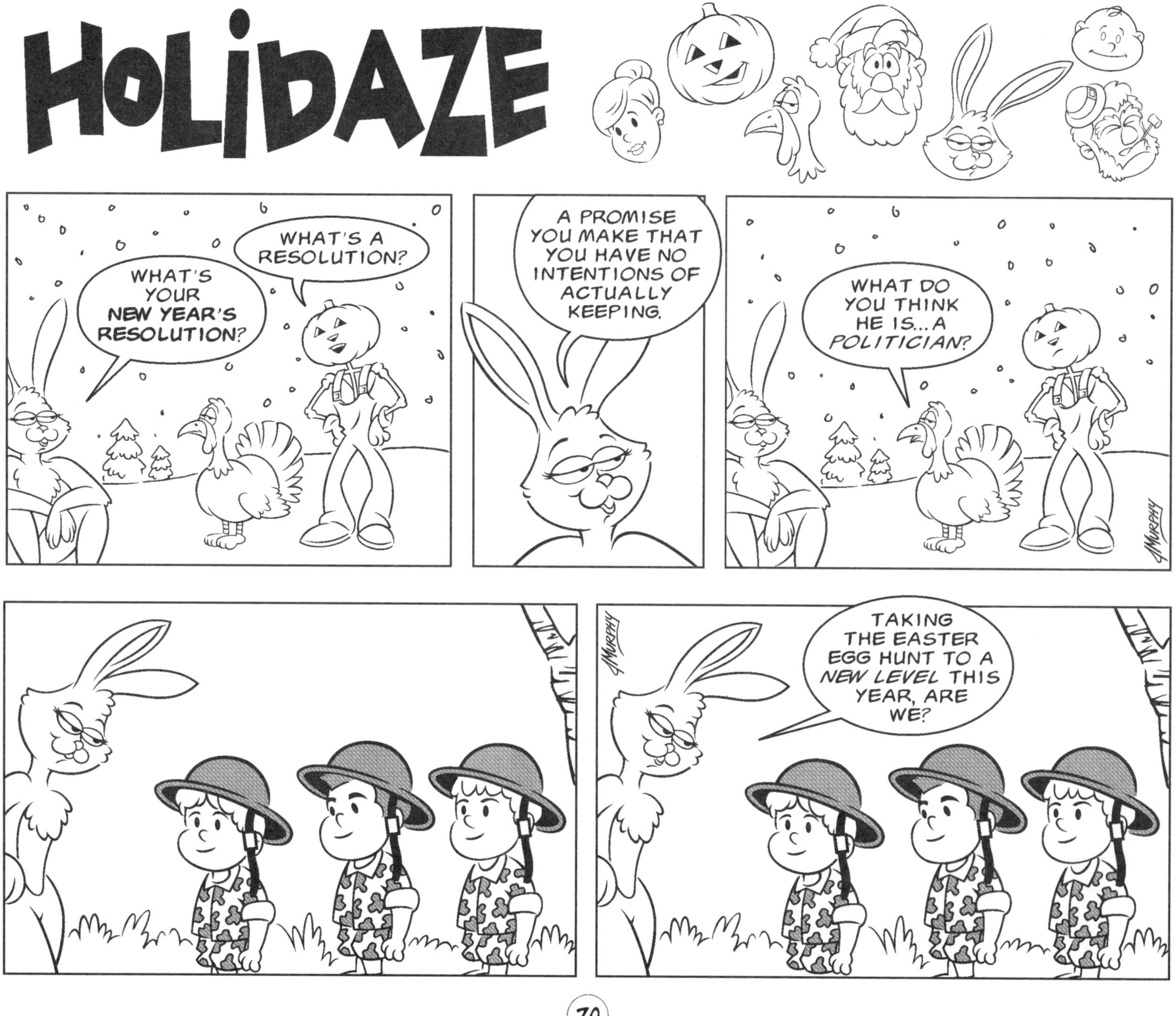
HOLIDAZE
WHAT'S YOUR NEW YEAR'S RESOLUTION?
WHAT'S A RESOLUTION?
A PROMISE YOU MAKE THAT YOU HAVE NO INTENTIONS OF ACTUALLY KEEPING.
WHAT DO YOU THINK HE IS... A *POLITICIAN*?
MURPHY
MURPHY
TAKING THE EASTER EGG HUNT TO A *NEW LEVEL* THIS YEAR, ARE WE?

HOLIDAZE

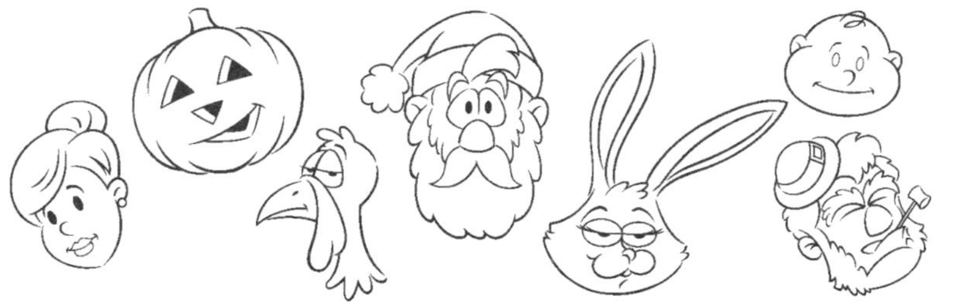

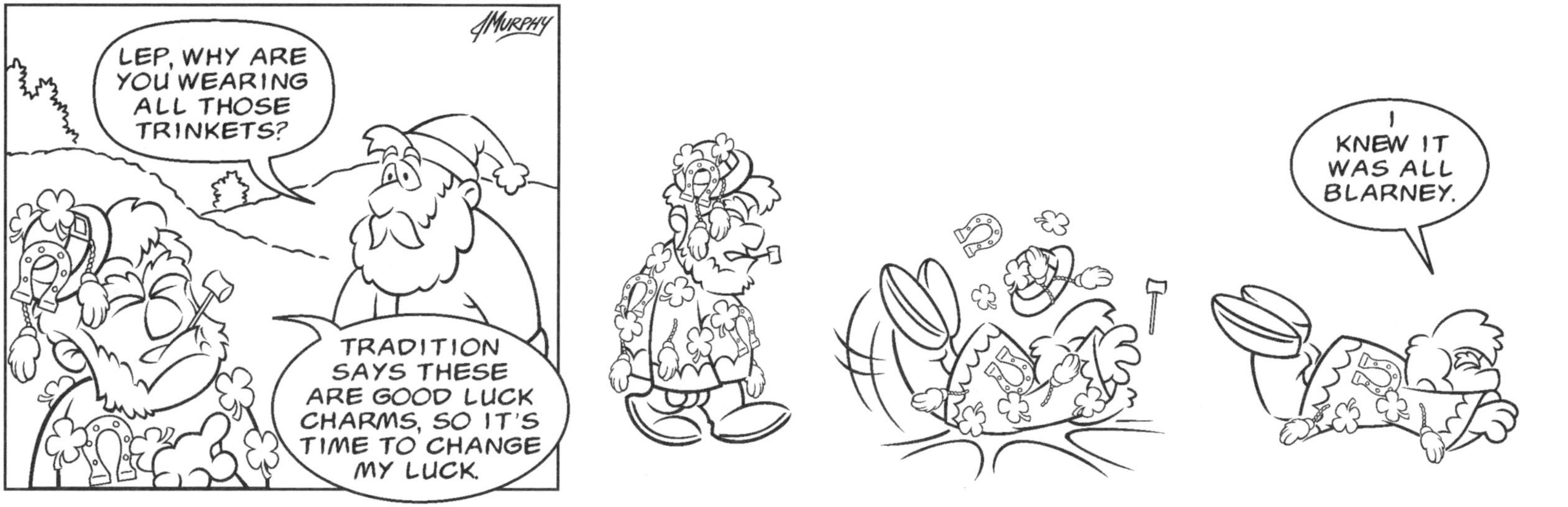
JMURPHY
LEP, WHY ARE YOU WEARING ALL THOSE TRINKETS?
TRADITION SAYS THESE ARE GOOD LUCK CHARMS, SO IT'S TIME TO CHANGE MY LUCK.
I KNEW IT WAS ALL BLARNEY.

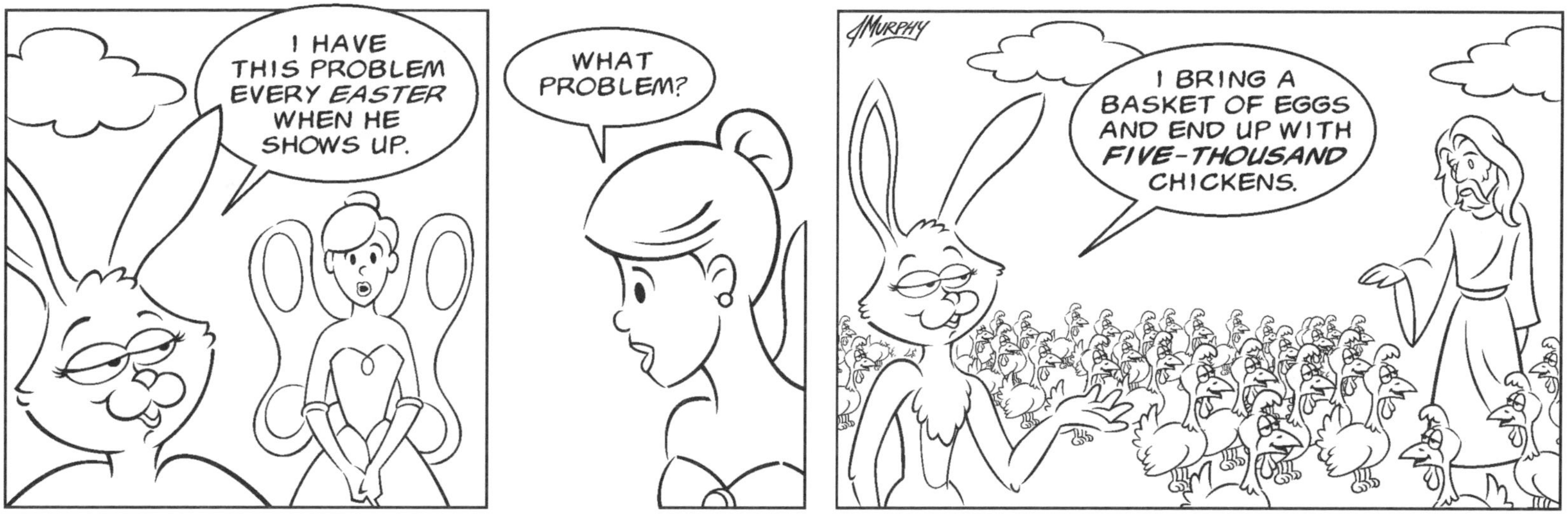
I HAVE THIS PROBLEM EVERY *EASTER* WHEN HE SHOWS UP.
WHAT PROBLEM?
JMURPHY
I BRING A BASKET OF EGGS AND END UP WITH ***FIVE-THOUSAND*** CHICKENS.

HOLIDAZE

BY JUSTIN MURPHY

BOBBY... TURN OFF THAT *TV* AND GO TO SLEEP.

OKAY MOM.

I SEE YOU WHEN YOU'RE SLEEPING.

WAIT... YOU'RE NOT SLEEPING.

TRY COUNTING *EASTER EGGS.* IT WORKS FOR ME.

OOOOO...

DON'T LOOK UNDER THE BED.

IT'S ALL ABOUT THE *IRISH* LADDY, ALL ABOUT THE *IRISH.*

INVEST WISELY. YOU ONLY HAVE SO MANY TEETH.

MOM!

HOW DO I TURN OFF THE *TV* IN MY *BRAIN?*

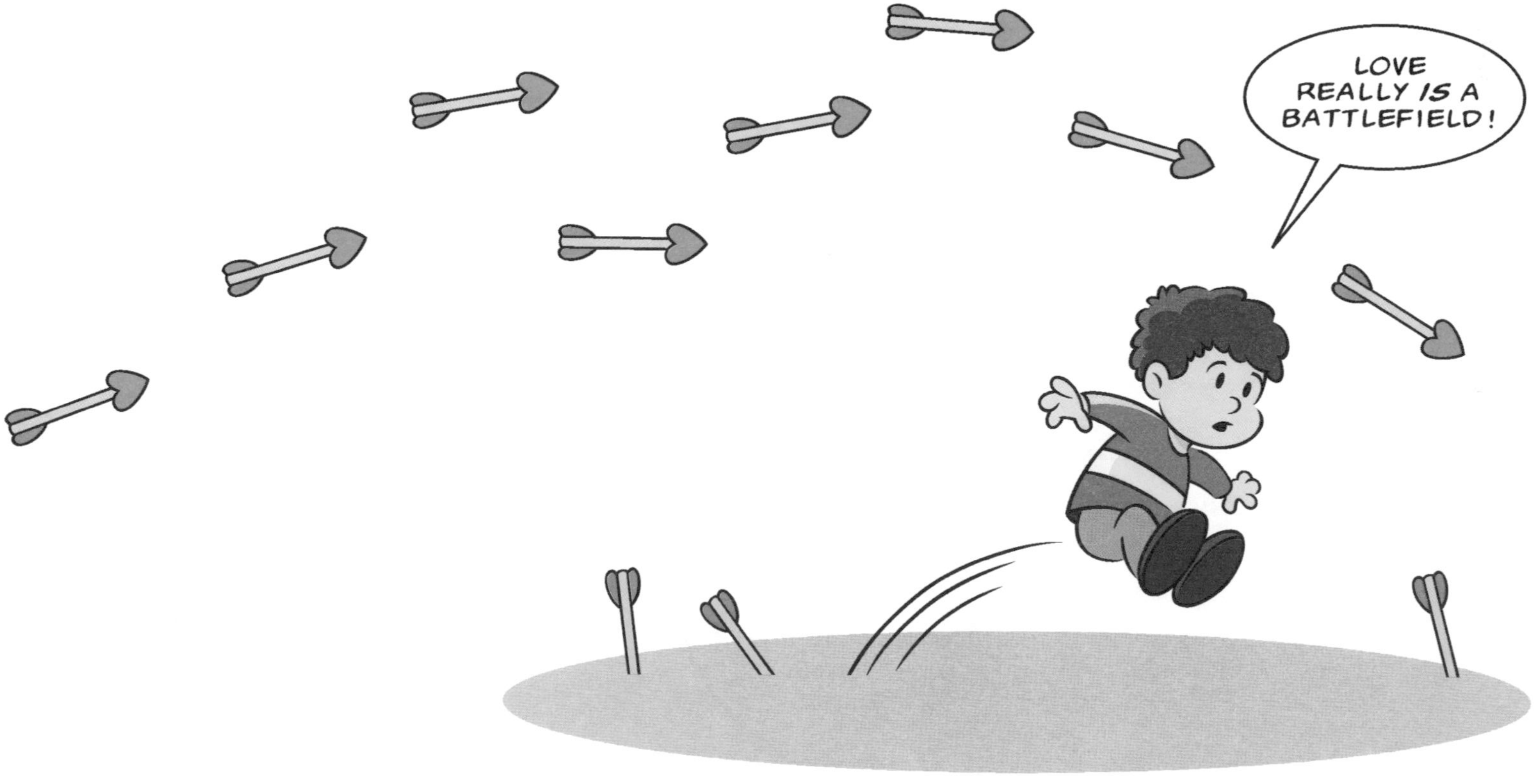
LOVE REALLY IS A BATTLEFIELD!

CHARACTERS

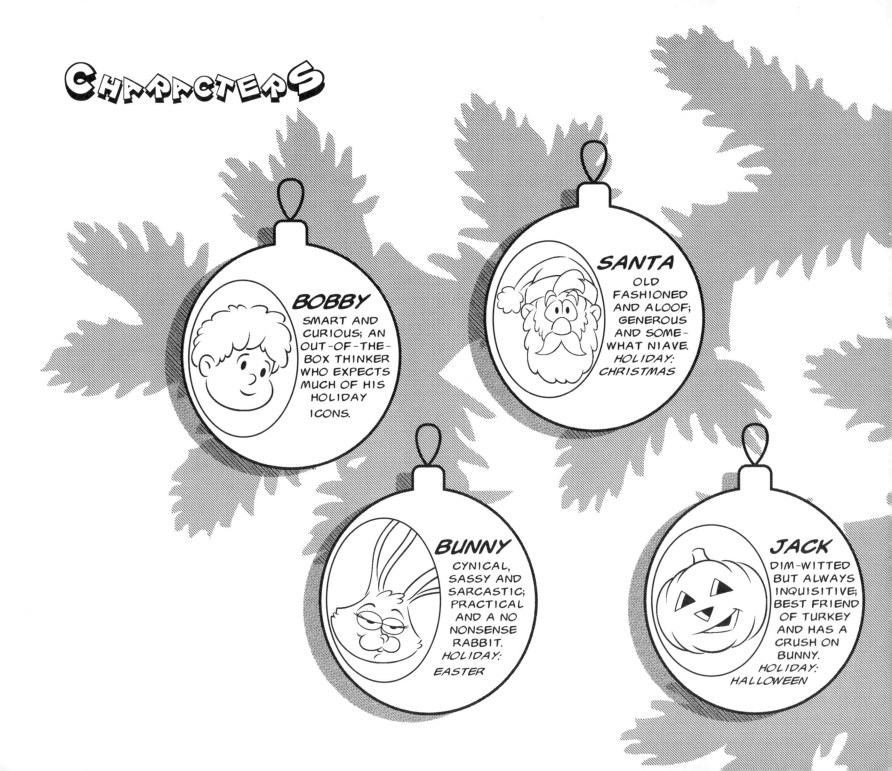

BOBBY
SMART AND CURIOUS; AN OUT-OF-THE-BOX THINKER WHO EXPECTS MUCH OF HIS HOLIDAY ICONS.

SANTA
OLD FASHIONED AND ALOOF; GENEROUS AND SOME-WHAT NIAVE. *HOLIDAY: CHRISTMAS*

BUNNY
CYNICAL, SASSY AND SARCASTIC; PRACTICAL AND A NO NONSENSE RABBIT. *HOLIDAY: EASTER*

JACK
DIM-WITTED BUT ALWAYS INQUISITIVE; BEST FRIEND OF TURKEY AND HAS A CRUSH ON BUNNY. *HOLIDAY: HALLOWEEN*

TURKEY
JADED AND SHREWD; ON A MISSION TO HAVE HIMSELF TAKEN OFF THE MENU.
HOLIDAY: THANKSGIVING

FAIRY
IDEALISTIC AND PURE; A FAIRY PRINCESS IN SEARCH OF HER PRINCE.
HOLIDAY: NONE YET, BUT TRYING.

CUPID
CHILDLIKE AND MUTE; CAN MAKE ANYONE FALL IN LOVE BY A SHOT FROM HIS BOW.
HOLIDAY: VALENTINE'S DAY

LEP
HOT-TEMPERED AND GRUFF; A PROUD IRISH LEPRECHAUN WHO'S ALWAYS READY FOR A STIFF DRINK
HOLIDAY: ST. PATRICK'S DAY

CHARACTERS

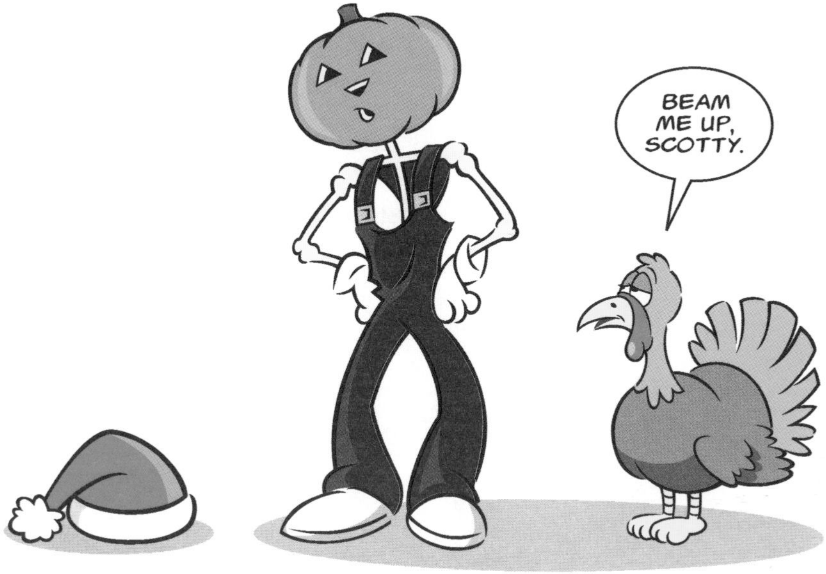
BEAM ME UP, SCOTTY.

JUSTIN MURPHY HAS A B.F.A. FROM JACKSONVILLE UNIVERSITY, AND IS CURRENTLY COMPLETING HIS M.F.A. AT THE ACADEMY OF ART UNIVERSITY IN SAN FRANCISCO.

HOLIDAZE IS JUSTIN'S SECOND ILLUSTRATED WORK FROM RAMPART PRESS. HIS FIRST BOOK, *CLEBURNE: A GRAPHIC NOVEL*, WON BOTH THE *2008 XERIC AWARD* AND THE *2008 BOOK OF THE YEAR AWARD* FROM FOREWORD MAGAZINE.

JUSTIN CURRENTLY LIVES IN FLORIDA WITH HIS LOVELY WIFE SHEILA & HANDSOME SON TREY.